Bi-Curious: An Erotic Tale

K.L. HALL

Bi-Curious: An Erotic Tale

Created with Vellum

Bi-Curious Synopsis

This is a novelette.

Candice Taylor is a sheltered, small-town girl who just transferred from an all-girls college to a co-ed university to finish her education. When the twenty-year-old newbie meets her roommate, Jasmine, she quickly gets a taste of her untamed lifestyle. The doe-eyed damsel's uncertainty of the unknown soon turns into curiosity as Jasmine brings out a side of her she never knew existed.

After spending one unforgettable night with sexy couple, Jasmine and Julian, Candice discovers she's no longer the timid girl she once was. She is immersed in the curiosity that piqued her interest from the moment she met her free-spirited roomie. Now, she's questioning not only her sexuality but her reasoning behind not exploring her sexual fluidity earlier in life. What will happen when her feelings become split between both parties? Will she have to choose who she wants, or will one of them choose her first?

One taste of Candice's innocence left Julian and Jasmine craving more. Yet, Candice finds herself having to choose between the man who makes her panties moisten or abiding by the girl code. When she learns the truth behind the couple's unconventional relationship, she'll have to decide whether she'll continue to explore the passion burning between the trio or bow out gracefully before she gets burned.

Chapter One

It was the *big* day. The day Candice moved from her grandmother's house in the small town of Barnesville, Georgia, to her first day at a co-ed university over three hours away. She attended a girls' college for two years until her grandmother finally allowed her to transfer. Candice was a short, fit girl with tan skin, deep-set, brown, almond-shaped eyes, thin eyebrows, thick lips, straight white teeth, and a slight dimple in her right cheek that offset the small mole on her left.

She took the elevator up to her new two-bedroom suite and opened the door to apartment 1204. She inhaled deeply, smelling the aroma of the faux leather navy blue couches. She ran her hand across the loveseat and smiled. She was going to love her new home. Candice looked around the apartment. A flat-screen TV was mounted to the navy blue accent wall, and a small white coffee table was in the middle of the floor with magazines spread across it. The stainless-steel kitchen was decked out in black, red, and white décor, and the pantry was stocked with food. She went to her bedroom and walked inside the ample open space. *I can do so much in here,* she thought.

"Hey there, welcome to our humble abode."

Candice turned around to see a slim, brown-skinned girl smiling at her. She had perfectly arched eyebrows, shoulder-length hair, brown catlike eyes, long eyelashes, and flawless skin with a nose ring in her right nostril. She wore a black and white baseball tee, dark denim jeans, and black and white Chuck Taylors.

"Hi, I'm Jasmine," she introduced herself.

Candice broke her trance and waved politely. "Hi, I'm Candice, your new roommate." Her voice rang with a heavy Southern accent.

Jasmine smiled. She liked the way her new roommate talked. "Well, look, I have to get to work, but make yourself at home, and we'll catch up when I get back, deal?"

"Sure!"

* * *

A few hours passed, and Candice had finished decorating her room with sky blue curtains, a calendar marked with colorful sticky notes for important dates, family photos on her dresser and nightstand, and a large, bedazzled mirror her grandmother had gotten her as a going away present. She placed her laptop on her desk in the corner and fell against her plush, sky blue comforter.

When Jasmine returned home, Candice was in the kitchen cooking. "I hope you don't mind. I got a little restless and didn't know where any restaurants were, so I made dinner. Do you eat chicken and rice?" Candice asked.

"Oh, that's not all I eat," Jasmine replied, smiling.

Candice ignored her comment, not knowing what she meant, and fixed her a plate. Jasmine hadn't taken a good look at Candice the first time they encountered each other, but that was when she noticed how beautiful she was, in the face at least. Her body was covered in baggy sweatpants and an oversized T-shirt, with her long hair flowing down her back. Candice brought their plates over to the dining room table and sat down.

"It's Candice, right?" Jasmine asked.

"Yes, but a lot of people call me Candy."

"Candy... I like it," she said, picking up a spoonful of rice. "Damn, girl, this food is the bomb! Where'd you learn to cook like that?"

"My grandmaw taught me everything I know. She always told me the best way to a man's heart was through his stomach."

Jasmine chuckled at how she said "heart" with her Southern twang. It sounded more like *hart*.

"So, do you have a boyfriend?" Jasmine asked.

Candice shook her head. "No, I've never had one."

"You've *never* had one?" she asked, shocked. "You mean to tell me, as gorgeous as you are, you've never had a boyfriend? Not even a fuck buddy?"

"No, I guess I'm just... different."

"Different is good, but how so?"

Candice sighed. "I know we just met and all, but... I'm a virgin. Men, well, they kind of scare me. I've been sheltered my entire life. I transferred here from a girls' college. This is my first co-ed experience ever."

Jasmine was shocked but intrigued at the same time. She smiled. "Hey, it's Friday. I'm meeting up with my boyfriend Julian at his frat house for his birthday party tonight. You're more than welcome to come."

"Oh, I don't know," Candice said reluctantly.

"Come on. It'll be fun, I promise."

"All right, well, let me clean up these dishes, and then I'll get ready."

"Girl, fuck them dishes. That's why we have a dishwasher! Throw them in there, hop your ass in the shower, and put on something revealing. We goin' out tonight!" Jasmine insisted as she hopped up from the table.

Chapter Two

Jasmine stepped out of the shower and rubbed baby oil all over her slim body. She wrapped a towel around her, and on her walk back to her room, she knocked on Candice's door to see what she was wearing.

"Everything okay?" she yelled through the door.

"Yeah, I'm almost ready," Candice yelled back.

"Well, open the door and let me see what you workin' with," Jasmine said eagerly.

Candice opened the door wearing a long, sleeveless, floral print dress with a floppy white collar. Jasmine tried to hold in her laughter. "Damn, girl, where'd you get that?"

Candice looked down, smoothed out the wrinkles at the bottom, and smiled. "I made it myself."

Jasmine didn't want to be rude to her new, saintly roommate, so she tried a softer approach. "Well, the frat house will be packed with guys and girls from all over campus. Take that off and come into my room. You can borrow one of my dresses."

Candice dipped her chin as her new roommate walked across the hall to her room and started rummaging through her closet.

"Wow, you sure do have a lot of clothes," Candice noted from the doorway. Jasmine jumped at the sound of her voice and let her towel drop slightly, exposing the piercing in her left nipple.

"Damn, you scared me!" she gasped before turning around to see Candice standing there with only her bra and boy shorts on. Jasmine could feel her pussy moistening between her legs.

"Oh, I'm sorry. I didn't mean to scare you," Candice said, covering her eyes. "I'll come back once you're clothed."

"No, no, no, it's okay," Jasmine assured her while pulling her towel back up. "I'm sure you'll see me completely butt-ass naked one of these days. I'm kind of a nudist." She laughed.

Candice blushed and lowered her hands. "Okay."

"I think I've found the perfect dress for you," Jasmine stated, holding a short, red dress. "It'll cling right to you like the sweet Georgia peach you are. Try it on!"

Candice took the dress and stepped into it, slowly pulling it over the curves of her body. Jasmine was right; it did fit Candice to a T.

"Perfect!" Jasmine exclaimed.

Candice turned to look at herself in Jasmine's full-length mirror and smiled to herself. "Wow, thank you so much, Jasmine!" she squealed. "I've never worn anything this... revealing," she admitted, running her hands over the sweetheart neckline and down the tight, crimson fabric.

Jasmine smiled, admiring her new roommate's natural beauty. It was captivating. Candice stood at about five feet, four inches tall, with smooth skin and her long hair pulled up into a messy bun. Her small but perky breasts sat perfectly on her chest, leading to a flat stomach and a nice, round ass. Jasmine watched Candice run her hands over her plump ass. She thought, *Who knew all that body was hiding under that God-awful sweat suit?* Jasmine found herself staring at Candice's ass, wanting to caress it. Hell, she wanted to bite it. Her pussy started to moisten again.

"Ooh, do you have heels to wear?" Jasmine asked, trying to regain her calm.

"I hadn't thought of those. The only heels I've ever worn were low, and those were only when Grandmaw and I went to the Easter Sunday service," she admitted.

Jasmine smiled at her innocent response. “Here, try these,” she offered, handing her a pair of four-inch, black, open-toe stilettos.

“I’ll break my poor neck in these!” Candice exclaimed.

“I’ll catch you if you fall.” Jasmine laughed.

Candice slipped on the heels and wobbled, trying to regain her balance.

“You know what? Those bra straps are throwing the entire dress off. Lose the bra,” Jasmine told her.

“Lose it?” Candice asked. “But what will I do for support? What if they come out?”

“Trust me. You’ll be fine. But if they do, I’ll catch those, too,” Jasmine said, laughing playfully. “Here, let me help you.”

Candice turned her back as Jasmine slid the dress down to unhook her bra. Candice shivered. “Your hands are so cold.”

“Sorry about that. It’s this damn air conditioner. It keeps me freezing. My nipples are always hard.” Jasmine laughed again.

“I’ll let you get back to getting dressed.”

“Yeah, go do your hair and makeup, and I’ll be in to check on you when I’m done.”

“Uh, sure,” Candice said hesitantly.

“Wait, don’t tell me you don’t know anything about makeup. I mean, not that you need it, but no lipstick, mascara, nothing?”

“Nothing,” Candice stated matter-of-factly.

Jasmine shook her head. “What am I going to do with you, girl? Take the red lipstick off my dresser and put it on. You don’t need much else,” she confirmed.

“All right.”

Chapter Three

When they arrived, Jasmine stepped out of her black Toyota Celica wearing a short, turquoise halter dress that showed the right amount of cleavage for her C-cup breasts, with four-inch silver heels. She smacked her shiny lips together and fixed her black, curly hair again in her rearview mirror. Candice wobbled out of the passenger side and approached Jasmine by holding onto the car.

"I don't know if I'm gonna make it with these on," Candice admitted, referring to her skyscraper heels.

"Don't worry, I got you," Jasmine assured her and grabbed her hand.

They stepped into the frat house, and all eyes were on them. Candice had never seen so many people in one place at once, except at her town's annual meeting once when the mayor was caught having sex with his horse.

"Do you drink?" Jasmine asked, interrupting Candice's train of thought by extending her a red Solo cup filled with cheap vodka and orange juice.

"Oh no, I've never," Candice admitted. "Grandmaw always said liquor was the Devil's juice."

Jasmine burst out laughing. "I'm going to bring out the wild side in you. Just watch," she promised before extending her the cup again. "Here, take a sip. If you don't like it, I promise you don't have to drink any more."

Candice agreed, took a sip from the large cup, and narrowed her eyes. "That's strong!" she exclaimed, coughing a little.

"Let me add more juice to it," Jasmine declared, pouring more juice into her cup. "Now try."

Candice took another sip. "Mmm, that's good."

"Great, finish that cup. I'll make myself another one."

The two had been there for an hour and downed three cups of Jasmine's cheap vodka and juice. Candice was starting to feel it.

"Jasmine, I don't know what's wrong with me. My... my brain is swirling around in my head, and I feel like I'm moving so slow," Candice confirmed.

Jasmine giggled. "That's called being drunk, sweetheart."

Just then, a tall, light-skinned man with a deep voice, wearing a crisp white Ralph Lauren polo shirt and camouflage shorts, came up behind Jasmine and grabbed her by her waist. "Hey, sexy, I've been looking all over for you."

Jasmine turned around to greet the tall man. "Hey, baby. Happy birthday! I want you to meet my new roommate, Candice. Candice, this is my boyfriend, Julian."

Candice could barely function, but she did manage to mutter "hello" and wave sloppily.

Julian whispered in Jasmine's ear, "Fresh meat?"

Jasmine smiled. "The freshest."

"Well, I'll leave you ladies to enjoy the festivities. Candice, it was very nice meeting you. I'm sure I'll be seeing you again soon," he stated in an assuring tone.

"It's my pleasure," Candice replied, being sure not to slur her words again.

As soon as Julian walked away, Jasmine grabbed Candice's floppy arm. "Oooh Candice, this is my song! C'mon, dance with me!"

"I'm not much of a dancer," Candice confessed.

"Oh, c'mon, loosen up. I know you're feeling the alcohol. Just let it move you."

Candice nodded and decided to throw her inhibitions out the window and live a little, if only for the night. Jasmine pulled her into the middle of the living room that was doubling as the dance floor for the night and started gyrating to the bass from the song blasting through the speakers while Candice stood awkwardly, bobbing her head and tapping her foot.

Jasmine laughed. "Just do what I do."

Candice watched as Jasmine rolled her body slowly to the beat and popped her ass in and out. She gradually started to imitate her.

"That's it," Jasmine said. "Now touch your body like this," she added as she ran her hands up her thighs, over her flat stomach, up the sides of her breasts, and over her neck. Candice mimicked her roommate's every move, enjoying her new sense of freedom. She ran her hands up her bronze thighs, over her round ass to her waist, and over the front of her B-cup breasts.

"Mmm. You look so sexy doing that."

"Really?" Candice asked curiously.

"Yes. You're really turning everyone in here on. Just look around."

Candice looked around the spinning room and noticed many eyes were on the two of them while also catching a glimpse of a few couples making out heavily on the couch, only a few feet away from her. She smiled a devious smile. "Let's give them something to stare at," she said as she turned around and backed her ass against Jasmine's pussy and started to grind slowly, just as she was taught. Jasmine followed suit and grabbed hold of Candice's tiny waist and pushed her pelvis area against Candice's bouncing ass.

"Turn around to face me," Jasmine declared.

Candice did as she was told, and Jasmine dropped low in front of her and ran her small hands up the back of Candice's firm calves, up to her smooth thighs, over her ass, and up and over her breasts. Candice let out a soft moan, something she'd never done before.

"You like that?" Jasmine asked. Candice bobbed silently, and Jasmine smiled. "Do you want to... touch me?"

Candice paused. Although under the influence, she had never been with a woman before. Hell, she'd never been with *anyone*. "I don't know... not here... not in public."

"C'mon," Jasmine insisted before grabbing hold of Candice's hand. "We can go to Julian's room."

Chapter Four

Jasmine led her curious roommate through the crowd of people, who seemed to all be making out with each other, but Candice let the thought go and blamed what she saw on the alcohol. When they reached the top of the stairs, Jasmine led them to the first bedroom on the left. Candice was shocked to see Jasmine's boyfriend sitting on the edge of his bed getting head from another female. He looked up when he saw them standing in the doorway.

"It's about time you showed up," he declared.

The mystery girl got off her knees and hurried out the door while Julian slid his stiff dick back into his boxers and pulled up his jeans.

"You brought my gift," he said, eyeing Candice.

Jasmine smiled and tried to pull Candice toward the bed, but she stood frozen. "What's going on here, Jasmine?" she asked nervously.

"It's okay. Julian just likes to watch. You're safe here. Just relax," Jasmine said, caressing her hand.

Candice made her way over to the bed and sat in Julian's warm spot as he sat quietly in the corner, never breaking eye contact with her. Jasmine stepped closer to her and brushed her hand across Candice's jaw.

"Your skin is so soft," she purred. "I'm going to enjoy this."

Candice could smell the liquor on her roommate's breath when Jasmine leaned in to kiss her cheek.

Jasmine sighed. "What can I do to make you more comfortable?"

"I don't know...maybe if we were alone," Candice said softly, making eye contact with Julian again.

"Julian, why don't you go get us something to drink? We won't get too intense without you," she promised, winking in his direction.

He got up to leave and closed the door gently behind him. Jasmine walked over to lock the door and joined Candice on the bed.

"He'll be gone for a while. It's just you and me now."

Candice exhaled slowly. "Can I ask you something?"

"Shoot," Jasmine answered as she crawled behind Candice and massaged her shoulders.

"Mmm," Candice moaned. "That feels good."

"I just want to make sure you're comfortable, Candy," Jasmine stated, kissing her neck gently.

Candice's body twitched, "I've never—"

"Shh, I know. I'll take good care of you," she assured her roommate. "Lay on your stomach."

Candice complied, kicking her heels off in the process. Jasmine straddled her and started to massage her back gently. "Can I pull your dress down... to get to the rest of your back?"

Candice nodded, and Jasmine slid her dress down slowly, reaching around to pull the fabric off her breasts and deliberately running her fingertips over Candice's nipples. Candice's breath hitched. Jasmine rubbed Candice's back slowly until she went down to her covered ass, where the rest of the dress was ruffled.

"Take your dress off so I can massage your ass, Candy," Jasmine instructed.

Candice stood up, revealing her breasts and erect brown nipples as she shimmied the tight material down to her ankles.

"Mmm, Candy, you're so hot," Jasmine whispered, running her fingers over her breasts. She reached out to caress Candice's ass through her boy shorts and then slid her right hand down between Candice's legs, noticing the dampness.

"Am I turning you on?" Jasmine asked.

Candice smiled shyly. "I've never done anything like this before; I don't know what's happening to me."

"Just enjoy it," Jasmine coaxed as she gently kissed Candice's soft lips.

Jasmine felt Candice's body relax as she slid her hands down her ass. Candice ran her hands over Jasmine's shoulders and down the front of her chest to pull down her dress. She broke the kiss to look down at Jasmine's full, mahogany-colored breasts and noticed her nipples were pierced. Candice licked her lips.

"Do you want to taste them?" Jasmine asked.

Candice looked up into Jasmine's catlike eyes and back down at her perky breasts. They seemed to be calling out to her. They were so round and perfect, almost seeming fake. She grabbed them. They were soft and jiggled in her hands; they were real. Candice lowered her head and slowly took Jasmine's right breast into her mouth, sucking on her hard nipple.

Jasmine moaned loudly. "That's right, baby, lick that nipple."

Candice flicked her tongue against the bar in Jasmine's nipple and grabbed her other breast. Just as Jasmine reached to put her fingers down Candice's soaking panties, there was a knock on the door. Julian had returned.

"Wait here," Jasmine insisted, pulling up her dress as she walked to the door.

Julian stood there with two red Solo cups in his hands. "Everything cool?"

Jasmine dipped her chin. "Just be cool, okay?"

Julian kissed her and reentered the room. He set one cup on his nightstand. "I brought you a new drink Candice, okay?"

Candice smiled slightly, wrapping herself tighter in his sheets. She leaned over and took a big gulp of the mystery drink. "That's smooth," she said.

"Good," he replied with a smile that revealed the dimple in his left cheek.

Candice smiled back; she was beginning to loosen up around him. She probably had the alcohol to thank for that. Julian sat back in the corner and took a sip from his cup.

"Proceed."

Jasmine turned to Candice and dropped her dress. "Lay back, Candy."

Candice laid back, and Jasmine crawled on top of her, exposing her barely clothed body from under the satin sheets. Jasmine kissed her, gently parting her lips with her tongue. Candice's eyes widened and lowered as she slid her tongue into Jasmine's mouth. Jasmine sucked on Candice's tongue slowly, teasing her while rubbing her thumbs in a circular motion over Candice's rock-hard nipples.

"Shit, Candice, you're getting my pussy so wet," she announced. "Do you wanna feel it?"

Instead of waiting for a response, Jasmine took Candice's left hand and placed it outside her soaked, red silk thong. "Rub on it."

Candice moved her hand slowly up and down the triangle-shaped fabric as Jasmine sucked on her nipples. Candice could feel a puddle forming in her panties, something she'd never felt for herself, only read about in erotic novels she'd snuck from her grandmother's hope chest when she was thirteen. Candice moaned. "I never asked my question."

Jasmine sucked hungrily on Candice's nipples, flicking her long tongue against her breasts and loudly slurping around her areolas.

"Ask away, but I'm going to eat your pussy now," Jasmine told her.

Candice remained still, unable to open her mouth as Jasmine pulled down her wet panties.

"Look who got wet," Jasmine announced with a smile.

Candice blushed with embarrassment and closed her eyes. Jasmine spread her legs and kissed her inner thighs, leaving a trail of spit from one thigh to the other and then to the top of her throbbing clit. Jasmine flicked it with her tongue.

"Ahh!" Candice screamed out.

"What was your question, baby?" Jasmine asked between licks.

"What... why, why are you doing this to me, and why is he here?" Candice asked, trying to catch her breath.

Jasmine stuck her tongue all the way inside Candice's pussy. "We're swingers, baby."

Candice opened her eyes to see Julian sitting back in the chair, stroking his large dick, eyeing her hungrily. Jasmine licked her fingers and slid one in between Candice's tight slit. Candice squealed.

"Damn, you're so tight, baby," Jasmine purred as she licked around Candice's glistening pussy lips. "You have a beautiful pussy, Candy... and you taste just like your name."

Chapter Five

Candice sat up on her elbows, tightening her ab muscles as she watched Jasmine lick her pussy. She reached down to move her hair to the side to get a better view, then moved her hands up to her breasts to caress them slowly. Jasmine's soft lips against her hairless pussy was a feeling she'd never felt. Candice had started to love everything about her new roommate. She began to pant heavily.

"Oooh, yeah."

Jasmine spat on her pussy lips. "Bounce up and down on my finger."

Jasmine felt Candice's walls loosen as she finger fucked her, so she slid another finger inside her. Candice's pussy muscles tightened around her fingers. "Talk dirty to me, Candice. Tell me the nasty, dirty things you want to do to me."

Candice paused. "I... I want to feel your breasts against my tongue again."

"Oh yeah, baby, what else?" Jasmine asked her.

"I want to... to taste your pussy," Candice admitted.

"Mmm, come taste this pussy, then."

Jasmine laid back, and Candice straddled her, kissing gently on her neck and then down to her breasts, where she sucked each of Jasmine's nipples repeatedly.

"Mmm, Candy, my pussy is calling you," Jasmine moaned.

Candice let out a deep breath and kissed down Jasmine's stomach to her freshly shaven mound. "I don't know what to do... will you walk me through it? I want to pleasure you."

Jasmine sat up on her elbows and gently pushed Candice's head down to her clit. "Lick it."

Candice did as she was told and licked her roommate's soft button.

"Mmm, do it again, just like that."

Candice licked Jasmine's clit again, this time flicking her tongue across it swiftly. She felt Jasmine's pussy leak juices onto her lips. She licked them and smiled. Candice had a newfound love for eating pussy. She spread Jasmine's legs and stared at her dark pussy lips and ran her fingers down them in a V-shape.

"Mmm, shit, Candy," Jasmine moaned.

Candice sucked on her clit and ran her hands up and down Jasmine's stomach and breasts to pull on her nipples.

"Oooh shit, yeah, lick it faster, baby!" she screamed.

Julian rose from his chair and sat on the edge of the bed as Candice continued to lick Jasmine's pussy. He reached over and started to caress Jasmine's breasts, slowly taking them into his mouth. He bit her nipple with his teeth.

"Ahh shit," Jasmine groaned. "Candice, let Julian touch you."

Candice lifted her head from in between Jasmine's thighs and lay down on her back. Julian began to stroke her skin slowly, rubbing his hands down the curves of her body. Candice opened her eyes to stare at him while he touched her. He was beautiful. From his smooth bronze skin, copper eyes, and thick eyebrows to his thin mustache, gruff voice, and soft black hair. She was enjoying her view. Julian lowered his head to suck gently on her nipples, teasing her by blowing on her wet skin, then flicking her nipple again with his tongue.

"Sit on my face," he demanded.

Candice was taken aback at his request, but obliged. Her connection to him was almost instant. Julian lay on his back as Candice straddled his face. He sunk his big hands into her ass to guide her pussy to his lips. He stuck his long tongue out and flicked her enlarged clit. She moaned.

"Mmm, Candice, I love looking at your pussy," he announced in a deep voice. "Look at me and tell me how good this feels."

Candice started humming moans through her teeth while staring down at him.

"Mmm, this feels so good," she said with a moan.

Jasmine slid Julian's boxers off as he continued to eat Candice's pussy. She shot some spit out of her mouth onto the head of his dick and drove it in and out of her warm mouth slowly while her right hand moved up and down his shaft. He instantly moaned.

"Shit," he groaned with his face buried deep in Candice's pussy.

Candice rose from Julian's face and fed her nipple to him. He made circles with his tongue around her areola and teased her nipple with slow strokes. Julian propped his head against a pillow as Jasmine sucked on his head. Candice kissed him passionately, then made her way down to lick on Julian's nipples, then back up to his neck and lips. She sucked on his bottom lip, then reached down to massage his thighs. He bit his lip.

"Put your mouth on it," Jasmine told her.

Candice's mouth dropped open, instantly drying out. "Oh no, he's too big."

They both smiled. "It's okay; I'll walk you through it."

Jasmine began to lick up the left side of his dick as Candice licked up the right. He moaned softly. "Kiss each other," he coached.

Jasmine pushed Candice's hair behind her ear, kissing her gently while guiding her hand up and down his shaft. "I'll hold the base. Just put your mouth on the tip," she told her uneasy roommate.

Candice opened her mouth and lowered it on Julian's dick as Jasmine spread his legs and sucked on his balls. They both began to take turns, switching his dick back and forth between their warm mouths and bobbing up and down while the other licked up the shaft and gently rolled his balls around in her hand. Candice stared up at Julian while her lips were still wrapped around his dick. He was staring straight back at her. She sucked harder.

"Mmm, yeah, that's it, Candice, tighten your jaws," he moaned.

Jasmine slowly lifted Candice's head off his dick and told her to lie on her back. Candice lay on her back as Jasmine slapped her breasts and kissed them. Candice caressed her shoulders as Jasmine sucked on her nipples. Julian stuck two of his fingers into Candice's pussy. She groaned.

"Give me your hand," he told Jasmine.

He took two of Jasmine's fingers and slid them into Candice's pussy along with his. They began to kiss, which surprisingly turned Candice on even more.

"Ride my fingers, so you can get used to riding my dick," he commanded in a baritone voice.

Candice slowly slid up and down on the fingers stuffed inside her pussy, grinding in circles as she leaned up to make out with Jasmine and caress her ass. Julian took his free hand to reach out and rub Candice's breasts.

"Mmm," Candice moaned.

He slowly slid his fingers out of her and rose to his knees to enter Jasmine slowly from behind as she began to eat Candice's pussy. He pushed his dick into her, stretching her insides as her ass jiggled against his thighs. The bed rattled as Jasmine threw her ass back against him while spreading Candice's caramel pussy lips with her hands and running rings with her tongue around her throbbing clit. Candice switched her eyes from looking at her to looking at Julian while rubbing her breasts. Jasmine reached both hands back and spread her ass cheeks open so he could go deeper. He grabbed her by her hips and pushed harder into her, watching her nipples shake against Candice's bare skin.

"Oooh, Candy, I love how it sounds when he fucks me. Do you want him to fuck you?" Jasmine asked.

"Mmm, yes. Keep eatin' my pussy, Jas. I'm about to cum," she moaned.

Candice threw her legs in the air, and Julian grabbed her left foot. She moaned uncontrollably at Julian's touch and ran her fingers through Jasmine's tangled hair as she came, soaking her face with glistening cum.

"Mmm, Candy, your cum tastes so good. Do you want to taste it?"

"Mmm, fuck. Kiss me!" she demanded.

Jasmine leaned forward to kiss Candice, sliding her tongue into her mouth. Candice moaned. Julian pulled his dick out of Jasmine and lay on his back.

"Jasmine, she's not ready yet. I want you to fuck her."

Candice's eyes widened. She wondered how Jasmine would fuck her or if that was even possible.

"Spread your legs," Jasmine told her.

Candice spread her legs, and Jasmine climbed on top of her, pressing her pussy against her roommate's, and slowly started to grind.

"Mmm," Candice moaned. "This feels so good. Your pussy is so soft."

Jasmine grabbed Candice's breasts and started to grind her pussy against her faster. "Ahh, shit, fuck, fuck, fuck Candice, your pussy feels so good!"

Candice reached up and grabbed Jasmine's bouncing breasts. "Oooh, I'm about to... I'm about to cum," she screamed, sucking in the air. "Rub your pussy harder. Mmm, yeah, fuck me, Jas!"

Julian stood up on the bed, watching the two of them bump their pussies together. He leaned against the headboard, sticking his dick inside Jasmine's open mouth. She gagged instantly. He held the back of her head as he fucked the back of her throat. Jasmine knew he would not stop until she came. She grabbed Candice's right thigh and pushed into her pussy harder. The slipperiness between the two made her pussy tingle, and she knew she was nearing her climax.

"Ahh, shit, Jasmine, I'm cumming!" Candice yelled.

Julian removed his dick from her mouth just as she came. "Oooh my fucking God, Candice, ahh shit!"

Their moans were like music to Julian's ears. Jasmine collapsed on Candice's body as she heaved in and out, trying to come down from her orgasm. They lay there naked in each other's arms, caressing each other.

"Candice, I'm going to penetrate you now," Julian announced.

Candice's armpits immediately started to moisten. She'd remembered how big his dick was when she put it in her mouth. She had no idea how she'd fit it in her vagina.

"Get on all fours," he instructed.

Candice looked at her roommate nervously. Jasmine kissed Candice's lips gently and started to caress her breasts again. Julian mounted Candice from behind and slowly slid his wide dick into her, stretching her virgin walls. Candice shrieked and gripped hold of the sheets. Jasmine caressed and sucked on her breasts to ease the pain. Julian had barely gotten his entire dick inside her when he stopped. "Shit, she's tight."

He pulled his dick out and reentered Candice's aching vagina. She had got used to having a penis inside her for the first time, which made her relax. The sex was even starting to feel good.

"Mmm," she moaned.

Julian smiled. He knew she was ready. Julian slid his dick deeper inside her, pumping faster but still gently. He reached around and grabbed hold of her breasts. "Suck on her nipples, Jasmine," he commanded.

Jasmine smiled, spat into the palms of her hands, and smeared her saliva onto Candice's jiggling breasts. She rubbed Candice's clit as Julian fucked her from behind, but Candice didn't want her nipples sucked. She wanted to eat Jasmine's pussy again.

"Lay down, Jasmine, and let me eat your pussy again," Candice told her.

As Julian pumped in and out of her with ease, Jasmine lay on her back with her legs suspended in the air while Candice licked her pussy. She blew gently against her shaven mound and kissed her clit slowly numerous times, making love to her pussy with her mouth. Jasmine moaned uncontrollably and grabbed a handful of Candice's hair in her hand while sliding her pussy up and down her face.

"Oooh, yes, you know just how I like it, baby, please Candy, make me cum, baby. I need you to!" she begged.

Julian slid his dick out of Candice and slapped it against her ass. "Are you ready to ride me now?"

She nodded before mounting him. While Candice rode his dick, Jasmine rode his face backward to face Candice. Jasmine ground her pussy against his lips while the meat of Candice's ass bounced back against his thighs. Jasmine reached out to grab Candice's waist to suck on her nipples again.

"Mmm. Shit. I can't get enough of your body tonight, Candy," she moaned.

Candice rubbed her finger down the crack of her ass, fingered her asshole with her left hand, and massaged his balls with her right while she rode him.

"Yeah, right there, girl," Julian growled before biting his bottom lip.

Candice bounced on Julian's dick as he ate Jasmine's pussy from behind.

"Ooh, Julian, baby, your lips feel so good against my soft pussy. I never want you to stop eatin' this pussy! Please make me cum. I want to drip cum all over your face!" she screamed.

Jasmine leaned forward to bite Candice's juicy ass cheeks and spat down the crack of her ass. "Mmm, yeah, I like that," Candice moaned.

Candice grabbed her ass cheeks and spread them apart. "Oooh, this feels so fucking good, Julian!" she screamed.

"Turn around and ride my dick backward," he ordered.

Candice began riding his dick like he asked while Jasmine came down to suck on his balls, slowly brushing her lips against them and then sliding her tongue up and down the lining of his sack. She took one ball into her mouth and then leaned up to lick Candice's enlarged clit while she bounced on top of Julian's dick. Candice reached back and dug her nails into his chest while he grabbed her hips, controlling her pussy as it slammed down on his dick.

"Tell me you love this dick, Candice!" Julian groaned.

"Ooh, Julian, yes, yes, I love this fuckin' dick!" she screamed.

"I don't believe you," he growled.

Julian pulled his dick out, making Candice and Jasmine get in the sixty-nine position. He hovered over them, watching them violently lick each other's pussies. He slid his dick into Candice from the back while she ate Jasmine's pussy, every now and then pulling his dick out and sliding it into Jasmine's mouth and putting it back into Candice.

"Tell me again," he ordered.

"Ooh, Julian, please, yes, yes, I love your dick so fuckin' much!"

Julian grabbed Candice's hair with his right hand and put his left on her shoulder while she rubbed Jasmine's pussy, sliding two fingers in and out of her.

"Ooh, your hard nipples against my pussy lips feel so good, baby," Jasmine moaned to her roommate.

Julian pulled his dick out and turned Candice around to stick his dick in her mouth. Candice sucked his dick while Jasmine licked her breasts, gnawing and flicking her long tongue against her nipples while staring at him. Candice started to jack him off with her mouth wide open.

"Ooh shit, I'm about to cum," he groaned.

"Come on, baby, cum right in her mouth," Jasmine moaned, fingering her pussy.

Julian grabbed his dick and started slapping it against Candice's tongue until cum shot out into her mouth and all over her lips. Candice licked her lips as Jasmine licked up Candice's neck and lips, sliding her tongue in and out of Candice's mouth so they could share his cum.

"Mmm," they hummed in unison.

Julian fell back against the bed, panting violently.

"Happy birthday to you." They giggled.

Chapter Six

Candice woke up in bed with no recollection of how she got there or the escapades of the night before. She rubbed her eyes, looked around at her surroundings, and then down at herself, noticing she wasn't wearing anything but her teal bed sheets. A sudden wave of embarrassment overcame her. *What did I do last night?* was the only question replaying in her head. All she had to do was ask Jasmine, but she wasn't quite sure she was ready to hear the answer. Instead, she decided to shower to clear her head, and maybe some of the night would return on its own.

With the swing of her arm, the covers blew off, and she turned to stand up. To her surprise, her legs wobbled like a baby deer trying to get its footing for the first time. She reached out to grab her dresser to stop the room from spinning. That's when she remembered the drinks. Oh, so many drinks. She ran her tongue over her teeth and could still taste the slight hint of vodka in her mouth. Inside, she cursed herself for getting drunk for the first time. Nobody told her about the horrible hangover she would endure the next day.

After a few seconds of standing as still as possible, she enveloped her body in her bathrobe and approached the bathroom door, where she heard singing on the other side. The door opened just as she was about to turn around and trek back to her room. Out stepped a naked

Jasmine. She dripped wet as a cloud of steam rushed out behind her to mesh with the cool apartment air. Candice immediately turned her head.

"Good morning," Jasmine chimed with a wide smile as her perky nipples greeted Candice's eyes.

"Good morning," Candice replied, still trying her best to divert her eyes elsewhere.

"You don't have to play shy with me anymore, Candy... not after last night." Jasmine smirked.

"I don't know what you're talking about. I'm fine," she assured her.

Candice could feel her heartbeat speeding up and the butterflies fluttering around her stomach. The longer she stared at her, the more memories flooded her brain of their special night. Her cheeks flushed as she smoothed her hands down the front of her plush bathrobe.

"Mmm, that you are," Jasmine mumbled, licking her full lips.

Candice shamelessly rolled her eyes. "Are you done in the bathroom?"

"Yep," Jasmine answered, flipping her wet hair to her back and sashaying to her room.

Candice couldn't help but let her eyes travel down to her roommate's plump ass. The way it jiggled with every step she took made Candice's body tingle all over, especially her pussy. She violently shook her head and walked inside the bathroom, hoping a shower would rid her mind of the savage thoughts.

"Am I gay?" she whispered aloud while staring at her bedhead in the mirror.

"You can't be gay, Candice. You had sex with a guy last night," she told herself.

Candice automatically brought her hand up to her mouth as her eyes widened. Reality had hit her harder than a ton of bricks. A virgin no more, a smile started to tug at the corners of her lips, and she began to admire the new woman she saw in the mirror. Soon, thoughts of Julian came crashing in like waves at the beach. Her fingertips glided down a trail of passion and bite marks from her neck to her breasts and navel. Those butterflies reappeared inside her stomach before she could turn on the shower. That time, they were turning against her. Nausea overcame her as she rushed to the toilet, dropping to her knees just in time. Jasmine overheard her from the other room and ran to check on her. She pulled her roommate's hair back and rubbed her back to comfort her.

"Are you okay?" she asked, concerned.

"No, I think I may have drank too much last night," Candice admitted, wiping her mouth with her forearm.

Jasmine chuckled lightly. "C'mon, let's go lay down so you can rest. That'll make you feel better."

"No, I just need a hot shower to bring me back around. Then after that, maybe I'll go lay down."

Jasmine bobbed her head understandingly and walked over to turn on the shower for Candice, who hovered over the toilet, afraid to move. Candice stood and looked in the mirror again, staring at Jasmine. She then quickly pulled out her toothbrush and mouthwash to brush her teeth.

"Step in, and I'll wash you up," Jasmine offered when Candice was done.

Chapter Seven

Naturally, Candice hesitated at first. After remembering their night, she was torn between feeling comfortable and nervous. She hadn't had enough time to unpack her feelings about everything because she was still getting flashbacks. Afraid for the butterflies to return, she simply nodded and stepped inside. As much as she wanted to, she couldn't hide her attraction to Jasmine's body. Everything about her was breathtaking. Everything was evenly proportioned. Her manicured nails matched her toes, and her entire body was smoother than a baby's bottom.

The soothing, warm water flowed all over her body as she leaned back against the shower wall and closed her eyes to let the water bring her back around. Jasmine pulled off her oversized T-shirt and stepped in with a loofah. Candice's eyes cracked open slowly, watching her lather it up and bathe her gently from top to bottom.

"Step up so I can rinse you off," she told Candice.

Candice did as she was told and let the water rinse the soapsuds off her wet body. Jasmine stood behind her, rubbing her hands across the back of her neck and shoulders while kissing her neck. A moan, no louder than a whisper, slipped past Candice's lips as Jasmine's hands continued to roam all over her wet body. Feeling Candice's muscles relax, Jasmine kissed her moist skin slowly as her hands caressed

Candice's breasts and played with her nipples. Her right hand glided across the top of Candice's ass and made its way between her thighs, stopping at the fold of Candice's pussy.

Instead of pushing her away, Candice turned slightly to look into Jasmine's dark brown eyes, then kissed her. A grin tugged at the corners of Jasmine's lips, and she kissed her back. The more Jasmine caressed her. The more feelings started to fill up inside both of them. Inadvertently, Candice had fallen for her roommate. She knew being so attached to someone she'd just met was not normal, but being with Jasmine felt right.

"Are you feeling better?" Jasmine asked, breaking Candice's train of thought.

"Much better."

"Then that means we can have some fun, right?"

Candice's eyes dropped to her feet as she smiled shyly. "What did you have in mind?"

"I think I need something to soothe my sweet tooth. You think you could help me with that?" she asked while simultaneously bending Candice over.

Within seconds, Jasmine's lips had latched onto Candice's tender pussy, sending a wave of chills rippling through her body. Her moans were so subtle and sweet that they started to make Jasmine's pussy drip like a leaky faucet.

"Mmm, Candy. How can you taste even better than you did last night?"

Candice's body jolted forward when Jasmine's tongue flicked her tight asshole. A new feeling that she surprisingly enjoyed.

"Ooooh, that feels so good," Candice moaned.

"Turn around so I can bury my face in that sweet ass pussy," Jasmine purred.

Candice rested her back against the shower wall once more and propped her right leg up on the side of the bathtub. Jasmine alternated between kissing and gently biting her inner thighs and then gently spreading her pussy lips to kiss her roommate's throbbing clit.

"Suck on my fingers," Jasmine coached, extending her arm upward.

Candice took two of her roommate's fingers into her mouth and sucked on them slowly. She moved her tongue around the base and then up over the fingertips and finally stuck both fingers deep into her mouth and swirled her tongue around them.

"Ooooh, yes, just like I taught you!" Jasmine moaned.

She slid her fingers out of Candice's mouth and then stood to her feet, sliding them past Candice's tight walls. Candice gasped, gripping the shower rod as Jasmine's fingers stretched her pussy.

"Ooooh, mmm." She wailed while trying to relax her wound muscles.

Jasmine peered down at Candice's wet breasts. They were aching to be sucked on. She seductively licked her lips and took her left nipple into her warm mouth to suck it. Candice tossed her head back in pleasure. There was nothing like a woman's touch, especially Jasmine's. It amazed her at how quickly Jasmine could turn her on.

"Mmm, yeah, suck my nipples, Jas! Oh my God, that feels so good!"

"Mmm, you like that?" Jasmine asked as she latched her lips onto Candice's other nipple while rapidly vibrating her thumb across her exposed clit.

"Yessss," Candice panted, struggling to catch her breath from all the adrenaline and passion coursing through her body.

Candice could hardly control her moans as Jasmine's warm tongue slid up and down her nipples. She began running her hands slowly up her thighs, over her ass, and up to her breasts, feeding them to Jasmine one at a time.

She had gotten so horny that she needed to taste Jasmine's pussy on her tongue. Candice pushed Jasmine's head back and slid around her so that Jasmine's back was against the shower wall.

Feeling a cocktail of emotions, she slowly lowered herself between Jasmine's thighs. She ran her hand up the back of Jasmine's calf as she propped it up on the side of the tub as hers once was. Even though Candice had never seen another pussy up close and personal outside of Jasmine's and her own, she was sure Jasmine had the juiciest and sweetest pussy in the world. The way her puffy lips sat up off her body drove her wild. With her eyes locked on the hairless pussy in front of her, she closed her eyes and leaned in. Just the clean smell of Jasmine made Candice vibrate with pleasure.

"I can't wait to taste you," Candice moaned.

All Jasmine could see was Candice's eyes between her legs as her tongue went to work, quickly flicking her clit and kissing all over her pussy. Jasmine grabbed a handful of Candice's wet hair and brushed it out of her face, so she could fully watch her enjoy her meal.

"God, I can't get enough of you," Jasmine moaned. "Your lips were made for this pussy!"

"Mmm, and your pussy was made for my lips." Candice hummed inside her.

Just watching Candice made it hard for Jasmine to control herself. She felt the makings of an intense orgasm surging through her body. My fingertips gripped the fabric shower curtain as her body quaked. She was ready to bust all over Candice's pretty little face.

"Ooooh, shit! I'm about to cum, Candy! Mmm fuck!"

Just as the words broke past her lips, her sweet nectar flooded Candice's mouth. Candice hungrily licked her lips as she snaked her body toward Jasmine's hard nipples. She kissed them individually and then stared deep into Jasmine's warm eyes.

"I want you to fuck me," Candice told her.

A wide grin spread across Jasmine's face.

"I have just the thing for you, baby. I'm gonna fuck that wet ass pussy so good! C'mon, let's go to my room."

Jasmine stuck her foot out to cut the shower off and pulled back the curtain. She took Candice by the hand and escorted them to her room, dripping wet. As soon as they got inside Jasmine's bedroom, something overcame Candice. They weren't feelings of regret or coyness. She was ready to take charge. Overnight, she'd gone from a timid virgin to a bona fide freak, and she loved every minute of it. She pushed Jasmine down on her unmade bed and straddled her.

"Let me rub you down with oil first," she insisted.

Candice glanced at Jasmine's dresser and grabbed a small bottle of lavender-scented baby oil. The sweet smell wafted past her nose while massaging it between her warm palms. Slowly, she began stroking her sticky hands over Jasmine's full breasts. Jasmine let out a soft moan that somewhat mimicked a whimper. She was falling in love with Candice. Once Jasmine's entire body was slippery with baby oil, Candice parted her smooth thighs like the Red Sea and inched down to her buttery smooth pussy. Her tongue had become a magnet to Jasmine's sweet spot. She'd simply become addicted to cumming and making Jasmine cum, too. Candice licked, flicked, and kissed her roomie's juicy clit, while Jasmine gazed down at her.

"Mmm, fuck, Candy! I thought you wanted me to fuck you. When you gon' let me take control?" she quizzed.

Candice glanced up as a smile parted her sticky, wet lips. "After I make you cum again."

Jasmine closed her eyes and let Candice do what she did best, eat her pussy. She relaxed into the moment and massaged her plump breasts while tugging at her firm nipples. "Mmm yeah, lick that pussy, baby."

Eager to watch, she tilted her head forward, tightening her ab muscles. She noticed Candice's toes curling and soon realized she had one hand between her thighs. Candice being a quick study, brought a smile to Jasmine's face. She knew she'd taught her how not only to please a woman but herself as well.

"Mmm shit, I'm about to cum again, Candice, don't fuckin' stop! Don't you fuckin' stop!"

"Mmm, cum in my mouth again, Jas!" Candice breathed.

The anticipation of her next release set Jasmine's entire body ablaze. She felt like a raging volcano about to explode.

"Ahh, fuck!" Jasmine yelled as she threw her quivering legs in the air. "Fuck!" she yelled again, trying to catch her breath.

Proudly stepping back to admire her work, Candice crawled onto the bed next to Jasmine as she rode out the wave of her orgasm. Jasmine turned her head and gently brushed Candice's hair behind her ear.

"Pop that pussy up in the air and let me show you what it is," she demanded.

After propping herself up on all fours, Candice watched as Jasmine straddled her from behind and slid her middle finger inside her calling pussy. She was so wet Jasmine could see streaks of her sweet juice sliding down her inner thighs. Jasmine carelessly chomped down on her bottom lip and then bent down to squeeze and suck on Candice's pussy lips, making a big smacking sound with her full lips. While Candice's sweet moans filled her room, she reached into her nightstand and grabbed her black strap-on.

Grabbing it by the base, she sucked on the tip and brought it to Candice's lips. Without needing Jasmine to say anything, she took it in her mouth to get it nice and wet. The corners of Jasmine's lips curved toward the ceiling as she watched her, remembering how they'd serviced Julian the night before. Secretly wishing he was around, she hooked the strap across her body and rubbed it up and down Candice's tight slit. As soon as the tip entered her, Candice gasped for air.

"Ooooh, shit!"

Jasmine firmly held the base of the dick and gently slid it in and out of her roommate's warmth to get her used to its girth. After a few strokes, Candice's body relaxed, and her soft moans filled the space again. Jasmine's fingertips gripped her petite waist and thrust her pelvis forward, fucking her harder.

Candice reached out, firmly gripping Jasmine's pillow with both hands. She could feel herself nearing climax when Jasmine reached around to rub her pulsating clit.

"Yes! Yes!"

"Does it feel good, Candy?"

"Mmm, yes!"

Excited, Jasmine pumped harder inside her, edging her closer to her climax. She drew back her hand and smacked Candice's bouncing ass cheek, mesmerized by Candice's cries of pleasure bouncing off the walls. A wave of selfishness fell over her, and she pulled out of Candice, not wanting her to cum on something she couldn't feel. She immediately replaced the strap with her tongue, craving her taste again.

Jasmine flipped her over onto her back and lowered herself in front of Candice's plump pussy. As sweet as Candice tasted, there was no way she couldn't tongue fuck her roommate's pussy every chance she got. As far as she was concerned, a working tongue was all either of them needed.

"God damn, your pussy is so beautiful!" Jasmine praised.

She slid her body against Candice's, kissing her neck and rubbing her soft breasts against hers. Jasmine slipped her tongue into her mouth, and Candice almost lost it. She moaned inside her mouth as Jasmine slid a finger into her pussy and finger fucked her to ecstasy.

"I—I'm! I'm—I'm cumming!" Candice bellowed as her words melted from her lips.

Moments after the body convulsions and the tingling in her toes ceased, the two cuddled up underneath the sheets. Jasmine lay behind her in the spooning position, kissing lightly on her neck. Experiencing feelings she never thought she would, Candice let out a moan no louder than a whisper. Thoughts of their erotic spree danced through her head, with sprinkled images of Julian here and there. Candice knew everything about Jasmine fucking her felt good, but it was nowhere close to the power behind Julian's dick.

"When is Julian coming over?" she asked.

"Later tonight, why?" Jasmine asked with her right eyebrow slightly arched.

"No reason, I was just wondering." She answered, turning to kiss Jasmine's cheek.

Jasmine let out a soft chuckle. "I think I've turned you into a nympho."

"I think you have, too."

Chapter Eight

About an hour later, Candice crept out of Jasmine's bed and crawled into her own, falling into a deep slumber. Later that night, she woke up to pounding on the door and quickly jolted up, immediately grabbing her head to stop it from swooshing around. She hurriedly put on her robe and went to answer the door. To her surprise and delight, Julian stood there looking delicious.

She studied his features, from the top of his wavy hair to the Nike running shoes on his size eleven feet, without bothering to speak. Although that was nice, it was the in-between that made her smile. How his muscles bulged effortlessly through the fabric of his shirt down to the dick print through his gray sweatpants made her cat cream.

"Hey," he greeted her with a wide grin.

"Hi."

Wanting to say more, she stepped back, and he walked through the threshold of what had become her and Jasmine's sex fortress. Seconds had passed, and she still hadn't found the words to say to him. Insecurely gripping her robe and pulling it closer to her body, she turned to walk back into her room. Unable to get him out of her mind, she pressed her ear to her closed bedroom door and strained to hear any conversation between him and Jasmine.

"You fucked her, didn't you?" he asked.

"We fucked each other," Jasmine replied.

Candice sucked her teeth when the sounds of their voices faded. Moments later, her senses heightened when she heard Jasmine's moans echoing through the thin apartment walls. She didn't know whether to be jealous or turned on. Leaning her head against the door, she closed her eyes and, in no time, found her hand between her thighs, slowly caressing her already wet pussy.

"Mmm, shit," she whispered.

The louder Jasmine's moans got, the faster Candice pressed her fingertips against her clit, rubbing viciously in circular motions. Just as she was about to fulfill her selfish desires, there was a knock on her door. Candice gasped, quickly sliding her hand away from her pussy and turning the knob. Her eyes widened with excitement when she saw Jasmine and Julian standing naked in her doorway. She swallowed hard, not knowing if she could do the things she'd done the night prior without being inebriated, but she was eager to find out.

Her breath hitched when Julian stepped into her personal space, towering over her small frame. Instantly, her palms moistened as she waited for him to talk or kiss her, whichever came first.

"Are you scared of me, Candice?" he asked.

"No, are you scared of me?" she replied.

A chuckle broke past his lips at her sassy remark. "A little," he admitted.

"Really? I can't see anything scary about me."

"Look, last night was the best birthday present I've ever gotten. You were perfect in every way."

At a loss for words yet again, Candice lowered her eyes from his intense gaze and instead focused her attention on Jasmine, who ran her hands down his washboard abs while he stroked his hard dick. A tingling sensation buzzed throughout her pussy, pinging each nerve. Jasmine sauntered over to stand behind her as Julian stepped closer, making her the chocolate cream filling in their Oreo. He gently placed his strong hands on her neck and pulled her lips onto his. His soft lips sent electric jolts surging through her body. She soon felt Jasmine's soft hands caressing her breasts and ass from behind.

The trio went to Candice's bed and got comfortable on her

disheveled sheets. Julian gently began sucking on Candice's breasts while gently laying her down. He didn't believe in wasting time, no matter what he was doing. If he wanted something, he went after it then and there. He spread her legs wide and extended his long tongue, touching her sensitive flesh. Just the tip of his tongue on her pussy drove Candice wild. He began sucking on her pussy lips and then her clit while Jasmine slipped her tongue into her mouth, then climbed on top to sit on her face.

"You know I need to feel your magic tongue again," she purred.

Without hesitation, Candice began lapping and kissing Jasmine's pussy while Julian serviced her down below. Candice used her left hand to smack Jasmine's soft ass and her other to palm Julian's waves, signaling that she didn't want him to stop. It became clear that she didn't want but *needed* them both. Julian stopped to roll his elongated tongue over Candice's dark nipples while gently biting Jasmine's ass. Candice's lower body jerked when his wide thumb pressed against it, then flicked across her clit.

Jasmine could feel herself about to cum once more as she bucked her pussy lips against Candice's glistening face. With her fingertips wrapped tightly around the headboard, her roomie's mouth game made her feel euphoric.

"Fuckkkkkkkk!" she groaned.

With his dick standing at full attention, Julian pulled Jasmine's lip onto it and watched her suck on it. His eyes were fixated on Candice as he watched her toy with her pussy. Jasmine moaned while she sucked and slurped on his dick, but even she couldn't distract his gaze. He knew who he wanted. Refusing to cum, Julian grabbed the base of his dick and slowly slid it out from between Jasmine's jaws. He was ready to pound Candice's pussy and Candice's pussy only.

"What's wrong?" Jasmine asked.

"Come here, Candice."

Confused, Candice simply replied, "Huh?"

"Yeah. What are you doing, baby?" Jasmine asked with her eyebrows knitted in confusion.

"She did such a great job last night. I want her to myself."

"Julian, you've never done that before."

"So fuckin' what? You can stay if you want, but you can only look, not touch, from this moment forward," he bossed.

Jasmine instantly became angry and jealous, not because Candice got Julian, but because *he* got *all* of Candy's sweet pussy to himself. In all the threesomes or foursomes they'd had in the past, he'd never banned her from participating. She didn't know what to do or say, so she exited the room. Julian walked over and closed the door behind Jasmine, locking it.

Still utterly confused and almost afraid to speak up, Candice uttered, "So, what does this mean?"

Julian quickly closed the space between them and wrapped his arms around her waist. "It means I don't ever want to share your pussy again. Not even with Jasmine."

Chapter Nine

"I ... I don't understand," Candice stammered.

She was torn between feeling guilty and feeling turned on. She put the latter aside and chose to speak up for Jasmine. She could only imagine how she would feel if the shoe was on the other foot. Words like jealous, livid, and insulted came to mind.

"But what about Jasmine? I don't think it's right that you just locked her out like that."

Julian huffed out a quick breath. "Sometimes I just need... privacy. Trust me, she'll understand."

He chose not to give her a chance to respond by gently tugging on her bra straps so they would easily fall off her narrow shoulders. As soon as his eyes locked onto her breasts, he reached around to unhook her bra and started sucking hungrily on her nipples. Candice willingly tossed her head back and enjoyed the way his tongue felt against her hard mounds. Julian wasted no time pulling her hand onto his stiff dick.

"I want you to taste it," he told her.

Candice obediently dropped to her knees and took the head of his dick into her tight, warm mouth. They both knew that the old timid Candice was long gone. Julian wrapped his long fingers around the back of her neck and watched as she pulled his length in and out of her mouth like a popsicle on a hot summer day. She flashed her sultry eyes up at him and then went back to concentrating on pleasing him. She admired his long piece and almost couldn't wait to feel him inside her again.

She continued to slurp and suck on him while picking up the pace. He began fucking the back of her throat so deep that she knew she would gag up more than air. Seeing the distress in her eyes, Julian let up and backed away from her.

"Come here," he beckoned, outstretching his hands so that she could get off her knees.

She eyed his wide stance and chiseled body, then placed her hands in his. Once her feet were planted back on the carpet, he scooped her petite body into his arms, locked his arms underneath the bend of her knees, and buried himself inside her. She quickly sucked in air through her teeth as her walls expanded for him.

"Ooooh shit," she huffed.

Jasmine stood with her back against Candice's bedroom door, listening. As soon as she heard the two of them fucking, she placed her hand in between her thighs and started rubbing her clit in slow circles. Just the sweet sounds of Candice's moans made her nipples hard. With every stroke Julian made, Jasmine slipped her finger deeper inside her, fucking herself at the same pace. It was as if the three of them were still connected, although they weren't in the same room together.

Julian walked over to the door and pressed Candice's back against it, fucking her harder. Hearing Jasmine's moans intertwined with hers brought a smile to his face. He knew how much Jasmine liked Candice, but he wanted her more. He felt as if he'd compensated for kicking her out by letting her get off to Candice. Once he knew she'd cum for the first time, he peeled Candice's back off the door and went over to the bed with her body clinging to his.

Changing positions, he flipped her body over and propped her up on all fours. He would dig into her pussy from the back, his favorite position.

"Tell me how good this feels," he demanded.

"It—it feels so good!"

"You like when I talk to you dirty?"

"Mmm, yeah."

"Call me daddy," he demanded, smacking her ass.

She never understood why men who weren't fathers liked to be called daddy, but the way he put it down had her willing to call him anything he wanted to be called. Every time a word slipped off his tongue, and his strong voice filled the room, her body quaked. He could make her cum just from the sound of his voice.

He pulled out of her and kneeled to lick her asshole. It was a feeling she'd never experienced before but enjoyed. Julian pulled her onto her side so that the left side of her delicate body was parallel to her bed. He hooked his arm underneath her left leg and pumped into her with slow, deep thrusts.

"Mmm, shit. You ready to ride this dick?" he asked, then lifted her to sit on his dick.

Lost in the moment, Candice started winding her hips and bounced her ass up and down on him.

"Stick your finger in my ass again, Daddy!"

"Oh, you like that freaky shit, huh?"

"Mmm, fuck yeah!"

He wrapped his large hand around her throat and thrust upward into her while his middle finger pressed against her tight asshole. She could feel her orgasm surging through her toes as she rocked her body back and forth against his girth.

"Shit! Don't stop! I'm ab—I'm about to c—cum!"

"Cum all over Daddy's dick, Candice!"

Her muscles quickly tightened and then relaxed within a matter of seconds, and her body became limp on top of his. Julian flipped her over onto her back and gently kissed her soft lips.

"I'm not through with you yet..."

Chapter Ten

Julian exited her bedroom and caught eyes with Jasmine, who was in the kitchen. Feeling the tension brewing between them, he walked over to her and pulled her into his arms.

"Did you have fun?" she asked, folding her arms loosely across her chest.

"Did you?" he responded.

She lowered her eyes to the linoleum flooring in the kitchen. "She's irresistible."

Knowing exactly what she meant, he agreed with a nod. They both knew the only reason he made her sit out on their bedroom romp was because she got to enjoy Candice all to herself before he'd gotten there. Figuring she'd suffered enough, he kissed her soft cheek and whispered in her ear. "She's ready."

Jasmine tried hard to tuck her lips but couldn't contain her smile. Candice had no idea what she was in store for. An hour after Julian left, Candice made her way out of her bedroom with a groggy look on her face. Julian's dick down had put her right to sleep. She walked into the bathroom and looked at her reflection in the mirror. She felt bad for giving in to the desires of her flesh, but there was something about Julian that her body craved. His dominant presence commanded power by making her knees weak and her heart quicken whenever he was around.

She splashed cold water onto her face and knocked on Jasmine's door. Not only did she want to apologize for letting a good, hard dick come in between them, but she also wanted some answers. It was clear to her that whatever relationship she and Julian had was far from ordinary.

"Come in."

Candice turned the knob and traded glances with Jasmine. She quickly lowered her stare to the floor as she stood in the doorway.

"I just wanted to... check on you, you know? Make sure you're okay."

"Why wouldn't I be?"

She shrugged. "I don't know... just about earlier and how all that happened. I didn't think it was going to go down like that."

"I'm a big girl, Candy. I'm just fine. Besides, I can't blame him for wanting you all to himself because I feel the same way," she answered, flashing a slight smile.

"Really?"

"Yeah, really," she answered with a quick nod.

"But how? How does that work if you're both in a relationship? Isn't that kind of like cheating?"

Jasmine climbed off her bed and stood in front of Candice. She was so close that she could feel her breath gently blow across her face.

"Have you ever heard of polyamory?"

"Like when a man has a lot of wives?"

She let out a light chuckle. "No, that's polygamy."

"Oh, so... what's that?"

"It's more common than you think. Let's see, how do I put this in a way that you'll understand? Julian and I are *very* sexual beings. Early in our relationship, we agreed to explore having more than one sexual partner, but instead of doing it behind each other's backs, we do things on our terms and open our bedroom to other people."

"Like an open relationship?"

"No. In a polyamorous relationship, we can have feelings for other people too. It's not just about the sex."

"So what we did... you've done that before?"

"Plenty of times."

"Oh."

"But none of them were nearly as sweet as you." She nudged her.

"Thanks... I guess."

Once again, Candice turned her eyes to the carpet and the chipped polish on her middle toe. It all seemed a bit taboo to her, but she kept listening.

"I'm serious. There's something different about you, and it's affecting both Julian and me."

"I thought you'd be mad at me... you know, for earlier."

"Mad? No. If you haven't figured it out, I'm unlike most girls. Plus, I like you too much to be mad at you," she answered before swiping her hand across Candice's blushing cheek.

Candice bobbed her head up and down to show Jasmine that she understood, but just because she comprehended it didn't mean she had to accept it.

Chapter Eleven

The next day, Candice walked on campus from her class while Googling the definition of a polyamorous relationship with her Beats headphones on, blasting Beyoncé. She was knee-deep in an article when she ran smack into someone. All she saw was a cup of brown coffee splattering all over the shirt of the man in front of her.

"Oh shit! I'm so sorry!"

She quickly peeled off her headphones and looked at the mess she'd made.

"No, it's my fault. I should've been watching where I was going," he told her.

"No, I was in my little zone on my phone. I'm so sorry! Oh my God, please let me buy you a new cup of coffee."

"I could use a new shirt instead." He chuckled.

Candice laughed softly and was happy that he'd taken things so lightheartedly. The crash had happened so fast that she didn't even notice she'd dropped her phone. She reached down to pick it off the pavement and saw the cracked screen.

"Fuck!" she yelled.

"You should have a screen protector on that."

"Huh?" she asked, frazzled and half listening.

Instead of responding, the man pointed to her phone. She shrugged. "Oh. Yeah, it was on my to-do list."

"Guess you can scratch that off now, huh?"

"Yeah, I guess I can," she said, blowing out hot air.

"I'm Dimitri, by the way."

"Candice."

He extended his sticky hand to her, and out of guilt, she shook it.

"Are you new here? I don't think I've ever seen you before."

"Yeah, I'm new... transferred from an all-girls school."

"Wow, this must be a culture shock to you with all this testosterone floating around campus."

She snickered before nodding. "Yeah, it's definitely different."

She looked into his eyes for the first time, soaking in his appearance. He looked good besides the dark brown coffee stain on his initially crisp white T-shirt. His skin was a sun-kissed shade of brown, and he had a head full of curls on the top of his head that tapered into a fade toward the sides and the back. Black tattoo ink decorated his left arm down to his wrist. He had juicy, pink lips and a set of white teeth to complement them. Perhaps what turned her on the most about him were his black-framed glasses. To her, they signaled education and class.

"What were you looking at that had you so wrapped up in your phone?"

"Oh, um. I was just doing some research."

"On what?"

She could feel herself blushing and then shook her head. "Nothing, just some stuff for class."

"Oh, okay, at least you didn't say porn or something," he joked.

"Oh my God, why would you say that!"

"You'd be surprised by the things I've seen around here."

"I can only imagine," she mumbled, reflecting on her conversation with Jasmine about her relationship. "I wish you'd let me buy you a new cup of coffee."

"How about you buy me a cup of coffee, and then you let me walk you back to your dorm if that's cool?"

She pondered on his offer for a minute, hoping he was just trying to be friendly and not pounce on her or anything sexual. Before her lips could speak, her head nodded, and the two started walking to the coffee shop on campus.

Chapter Twelve

The two talked for two hours about their majors, campus life, and hobbies. Candice enjoyed his company and hadn't laughed that hard in a long time. Being around a man who didn't make her fumble over her words or feel weak at the knees was nice. She felt comfortable around him. When they got to her building, she stopped and turned to him.

"Well, this is my stop. It was nice hanging out with you today."

"Yeah, I enjoyed myself. Hopefully, we can do it again sometime. I'll be sure to throw an extra shirt in my book bag," he joked.

His joke made Candice grin wide. "Yeah, we can hang out again."

"Cool, well, I'll see you around."

Dimitri turned to leave, and Candice turned in the other direction to walk into her building. She heard Jasmine's moans bouncing off the walls when she entered her apartment. Candice wondered how Jasmine fit going to class into her extensive sex schedule. She hadn't been her roommate long, but she'd yet to see her pick up a book or attend a lecture. Figuring it was none of her business, she shook it off and retreated to her room.

She tossed her bookbag onto the floor and kicked off her shoes. As soon as she flopped back against her bed, her phone dinged. She'd gotten a friend request from Dimitri on Facebook. Before adding him, she scrubbed his profile, trying to see all she could. Once she clicked the accept button, she went back to her research. She read that being in a polyamorous relationship was all about respect and keeping the lines of communication open. She hadn't seen that with the stunt Julian pulled the night before, but figured by the sounds of Jasmine's headboard knocking against the wall, the two of them had kissed and made up.

As soon as she went to lock her phone, it dinged again. She'd gotten a message from Dimitri.

Dimitri Booker: Hey, I hope you don't think it's weird that I tracked you down on social media. I just forgot to ask for your number earlier.

Candice Taylor: Yeah, it's kind of weird, to be honest, but it's cool. How about you give me your number instead?

Dimitri Booker: Sure, no problem. 680-098-0001.

Candice Taylor: Got it.

She didn't know if she intended to text him, but he was nice to hang out with. A loud huff escaped her lips as she tossed her phone beside her. She closed her eyes, and images of her and Julian started dancing through her head. Her eyes shot open when she heard a set of knuckles colliding against her door. She slid off the bed and cracked it open. To her surprise, Julian stood there.

"Hey," she greeted him.

"Do you have plans later tonight?"

"Um, no. Why?"

"I want to take you somewhere."

"Take me somewhere, like on a date?" she asked for clarity.

"If that's what you want to call it, sure, it's a date."

Candice's mouth suddenly filled with cotton, and she couldn't speak. She understood the parameters of Julian and Jasmine's relationship a bit more, but still didn't feel comfortable going on a date with her roommate's man.

"Um—"

He cut her off. "I'll be by to pick you up at nine."

Julian left her standing in her doorway with her dry mouth hanging wide open. She wanted to go to Jasmine and tell her what had just happened or ask for permission even, but she didn't. She didn't want to be the one running to tell or apologize every time something foreign to her transpired. Instead, she turned on her heels and went to the closet to find something to wear. She wanted something that said she was sexy, but not a man-stealing slut. After fifteen minutes of sorting through clothes, she settled on a plain black dress. It wasn't very sexy, but it did hug her body in all the right ways.

After she got dressed, she caught Jasmine coming out of the bathroom and automatically felt terrible. She quickly slapped her hand across her lips when she felt a severe case of word vomit about to spew out. Jasmine had on a black teddy and a pair of strappy black heels. Her hair flowed down her back, and her makeup was on point.

"You going out?" Candice asked.

"Yup!"

"Where to?"

"My favorite spot," she answered casually, pulling a jacket over her body and buttoning it shut.

"Oh, okay."

"And what about you? You going somewhere?"

"Yeah, I—I think so. Julian kinda asked me to go somewhere with him earlier today."

"And what did you say?"

"I didn't get the chance to tell him yes or no, but if you don't want me to go, I won't."

Jasmine walked over to Candice, placed both hands on her soft face, and pulled her lips onto hers.

"He asked. I said it was fine already. Have fun. I'll see you later."

Chapter Thirteen

Julian showed up on time, and Candice's underarms moistened. Her heels sunk into the carpet underneath her as she walked over to get the door. As soon as she opened it, his wide smile greeted her.

"Hey." She smiled.

"Hey. You ready?"

She nodded. "Yeah."

"You got your ID with you, right?"

"Yeah, I do."

"Good. C'mon, let's go."

She grabbed her purse and followed him to his car. He pressed the unlock button and opened the passenger-side door for her.

"Thanks."

Once inside, she let her stiff back relax against the black leather seat and slumped down a little. Now that she'd gotten some background information on his relationship from Jasmine, she couldn't help but be interested in his point of view of it all. It wasn't like Candice to pry into anyone's business, but they had made it their business to rope her in, so she felt well within her right.

"I have a question," she announced, glancing over at Julian as he zipped through traffic on the interstate.

"Let me guess. You want to know what's up with me and Jasmine, right?"

"Y—yeah, I do."

"What all has she told you so far?"

"What makes you think I've asked her?"

"You don't strike me as the uninquisitive type, Candice."

The way her name fell off his tongue made her tighten her legs together, and for a second, she lost her train of thought. When Julian didn't hear her speak up immediately, he continued his statement.

"I fuck other women, and I've watched other men fuck Jasmine, but she's my heart. What we have, it just works."

"So, you *do* love her?"

"I do."

"But what if she loved someone else? What would that mean to you?"

"As long as her love for me doesn't change, I'm fine. I learned long ago that Jasmine's heart is too big to love one person, whether it's another man or somebody like you."

"Me?"

"I see the way she looks at you."

Blushing, Candice immediately turned her attention away from him. "What do you mean?"

"You have feelings for her too."

Feeling too overwhelmed to speak, she simply nodded.

"Just so you know, even though I meant what I said to you last night, I would never make you choose between us," he assured her.

"Good, because I would never want to."

The car fell silent, and she turned her attention out the window. It was the first time since she'd been in the car with him she wondered where exactly they were going. He'd gotten her train of thought so off-track that she hadn't bothered to ask.

"Where are we going again?" she spoke up.

"It's a surprise."

"I've never been one for surprises."

"Me either, but something tells me you'll enjoy this one."

The confidence in his tone made her relax and enjoy the scenery around her. Thirty minutes later, Julian parallel-parked on the side of the street and turned to look at Candice.

"Are you ready?"

"Yeah, I think so."

"Put this on," he instructed, handing her a black silk scarf.

She took the smooth fabric in her hand and looked down at it. "What's this for?"

"Trust me. You're going to want to put it on."

She put the scarf against her eyes, and Julian gently tied it behind her head. He exited the car to act as her eyes as they crossed the street. Candice could only rely on her other four senses to get her by so she wouldn't have a meltdown before discovering the big surprise. She heard Julian knock in a specific way, nothing like a general knock on a door. Her ears perked up when she heard an unfamiliar voice.

"Punch in the code."

She heard four beeps, and the door opened, sending cool air flushing over her skin. Julian wrapped his hand in hers and gently guided her inside. Once inside, he dropped her hand and wrapped his arms around her waist.

"How much further?" she asked.

"A few more steps," he whispered in her ear.

Candice followed his instructions and kept walking until he tugged back on her waist.

Without a countdown or asking if she was ready, she felt him untie the scarf from around her eyes. What she saw before her eyes was more than she could ever imagine. There were people she'd never seen before dancing naked, fucking, sucking, and watching others. As shocked as she was, her heart did a joyous backflip when she saw Jasmine walking toward them.

"Surprise." She smiled and pulled Candice's lips onto hers.

"What is this place?"

"Welcome to The Haven, Candy."

Chapter Fourteen

Candice's eyes scanned the room again, letting all the sexual freeness before her soak in. There was a woman in a cage in the far left corner. She wore a collar and matching thigh-high leather boots. The two of them caught eyes, and as uncomfortable as Candice thought she looked, she could see the sex in her stare. There were two couples to her right; both women stood up with every part of their bodies attached to a rope-like they were being crucified.

There were screams of pain and pleasure radiating throughout the secret place as people enjoyed being treated like human pets.

Jasmine took her by the hand, and Julian never let go of her waist. It was like she was floating and not controlling her body. She almost felt like she was in a dream. Jasmine led the three of them into a private area. There were no doors, only sheer blush-colored curtains surrounding a large king-size bed. Candice sat on the edge of the bed while Jasmine and Julian sat on opposite sides of her.

"How are you feeling?" Jasmine asked.

"Overwhelmed."

"That's normal. I was the same way the first time Julian brought me here."

"What is this place? Do people just come here to have sex with other people?"

"It's a place where people come to be free, Candice," Julian answered ahead of Jasmine.

She watched Jasmine get up to pour them all a drink. She handed Candice a cup and immediately tossed the clear liquor down her throat. She needed something to make her calm down and fast.

"Slow down... we've got all night," Julian told her while kissing her shoulder.

The feeling from his soft kisses mixed with the liquor coursing through her system made her muscles relax almost instantly. His strong hands started to massage her shoulders, and she let her eyes fall shut. Seconds later, she felt warm fingertips over her skin, sending chills racing through her body.

"Tonight is all about you, and remember, you don't have to choose," Julian whispered in her ear.

"Good, because I want you," she confessed, opening her eyes and then placing her lips against his. She then stood to her feet and made her way over to grab Jasmine's hand. "And I want you, too."

A smile parted Jasmine's lips as she slid her jacket off her shoulders, revealing her black lace teddy. Her skin seemed to sparkle under the dim lighting in their secluded section. She'd been fantasizing about the moment that the three of them would be able to have fun again, and by the way Candice had opened up like a freshly bloomed flower, she knew she wasn't alone.

Jasmine ran her hand up Candice's shoulders, stopping at her neck, and pulled her lips onto hers. Before falling too deep into the kiss, Candice stepped back. An apprehensive look fell over her face as she looked around.

"Wait. What about all the people?"

Jasmine hooked her index finger underneath Candice's chin and shook her head. "Close your eyes. Nobody is here but the three of us."

Candice felt Jasmine's lips pressed against hers again and allowed herself to submerge into the moment fully. She soon felt Jasmine's small hands caressing her breasts through her bra.

"I missed these. You have the perfect tits," Jasmine purred.

A smile crept across Candice's face as she placed her hands on Jasmine's breasts. Even through the fabric of the negligee, she could feel

Jasmine's soft skin. Candice peeled the spaghetti straps off Jasmine's shoulders and sucked on her roomie's sweet, dark nipples that resembled Hershey's Kisses. Jasmine tossed her head back and let her mouth gape open as Candice flicked her hard mounds with her tongue.

"Mmm, shit."

Jasmine slid her hand between Candice's warm thighs and pulled her black lace panties to the side. She felt the wetness on her fingertips and licked her lips. Her mouth watered at the thought of tasting Candice again. She hurriedly put her index finger in her mouth, savoring the taste.

"Taste like... candy," she whispered to Candice with a smile.

Candice continued to gently suck on Jasmine's nipples while Julian came up behind her and simultaneously pulled down the straps to her dress and bra. As soon as her breasts were free, he massaged them. Jasmine pressed her exposed chest against Candice's and started rubbing her nipples against hers.

"Oh my God, I love your fuckin titties," Jasmine hummed.

Jasmine extended her long tongue to flick her nipple, and Candice joined in, sucking on it. Soon, their tongues were swirling around each other's mouths. Almost ready to explode from the foreplay alone, Candice dropped to her knees and lifted Jasmine's lingerie. She wasn't surprised that there were no panties to take off; this only made her job easier.

"I wanna taste you so bad," she confessed.

Jasmine eagerly propped her leg up on the edge of the bed and stood while Candice lapped away at her pussy.

"Yeah, that's right, eat that pussy real good. Mmm, shit. Just like that," Jasmine coached.

She spread her legs wider and wildly ran her fingers through Candice's hair. As much as Julian enjoyed watching the two of them get off on each other, he wanted to be a part of the special moment every step of the way. He walked behind Jasmine and started caressing her ass while kissing her neck. She gasped when she felt his wet finger enter her asshole.

"Mmm, fuck, Daddy!" she panted.

Candice's tongue lay flat against her roomie's clit as she moved it in slow circles. She could lick and suck on Jasmine's clit for hours and never get tired.

"Ride my face," Candice demanded while walking over to the bed and lying flat on her back.

Jasmine mounted her lips in the reverse cowgirl position so that Candice could eat her pussy from the back and immediately started grinding against her tongue. Julian climbed on top of the bed between Candice's legs and started sucking on Jasmine's nipples, edging her closer and closer to her climax.

"Ooooh fuck! Don't stop! Don't either of you dare fuckin' stop!" she screamed.

The louder Jasmine moaned, the faster Julian and Candice licked and sucked on her most sensitive areas. They were both determined to send her flying into ecstasy.

"Tongue fuck this pussy, mmm, yeah, just like that!" she groaned while winding her hips in fast circles.

Jasmine's body quivered within seconds, and she released her sweet cream on Candice's lips.

"Fuck!" she panted, trying to catch her breath.

Feeling proud of herself, Candice opened her eyes and looked around her. Couples surrounded the trio on the other side of the sheer curtains, watching their "private" freak show. It was the first time she didn't care about being watched or what people thought. All she wanted to do was cum over and over again.

Jasmine bent down and kissed Candice's sweet spot through her drenched panties, then slid them off and tossed them onto the floor. "You won't be needing these anymore."

She turned to face Candice and couldn't help but kiss her glistening, pouty lips again. Candice gently parted her mouth to receive Jasmine's warm tongue, then quickly pulled her dress over her head and tossed it onto the floor, along with her bra. Jasmine swiped her hand against Candice's sweet spot and smiled. Without speaking, Jasmine spread Candice's legs wide and started grinding her wet pussy against Candice's. The feeling was almost electric.

"Ooooh fuckkkkkkkk," Candice moaned.

Instantly, her muscles tensed up and went weak at the same time. She didn't know how to explain it. All she knew was that it felt good. She glanced over at Julian, who had relieved himself of his clothes. He stood on the opposite side of the bed, stroking his long, hard dick. Candice's teeth sliced into her bottom lip, admiring how sexy he looked watching them.

"Come here," she beckoned.

Julian made his way over to her as his eyes pierced into hers. His gaze traveled down to her naked body lying underneath Jasmine's. "Your body is fucking amazing," he told her.

Candice smiled as he bent down to kiss her. Jasmine continued to ride her, sliding her fingertips over Candice's nipples, which kept them rock hard.

"Fuck her until she cums, Jas. Don't stop until she cums!" he demanded.

Julian smacked Jasmine's ass, which made her buck against Candice's slippery pussy lips harder. Seconds later, Candice felt the familiar vibrating sensation coursing through her lower body, telling her brain she was about to hit the jackpot. Her mouth gaped open, sucking in air while her fingertips dug into Jasmine's plump ass.

"Mmmm, shit! I'm—I'm about to—to cu-cum!" Candice screamed.

As soon as she climaxed, Jasmine climbed off her, and Julian pulled her pussy onto his lips to taste her. He lifted her dainty body off the bed and wrapped her legs around his neck so that he could eat her pussy standing up.

"J—Julian, Ooooh shit. Ooooh my God!" she moaned.

He rolled his tongue against her throbbing clit. "Call me Daddy," he demanded.

He buried his tongue deep inside Candice while Jasmine bent down to suck his dick. While in her euphoric world, Candice started bucking against Julian's face, edging on to another climax. Unbeknownst to her, their night was just getting started.

After a few more lashes of his wet tongue, Julian gently laid Candice down on the bed, leaving the lower half of her body hanging off the edge. His thumb flicked across her clit, and she jolted forward. He smiled and slid his dick inside her while rubbing on her clit. He pressed hard against it to make her cum for a third time.

"Shiiiiiiiittttttt." She quivered.

Candice's back arched, and she gasped when he abruptly pulled out of her. He climbed beside her on the bed, locked his hand around her jaw to open her mouth, and slid his dick against her tongue. The taste of Julian's dick in her mouth made her rub her clit again, just like he had. Jasmine aided Candice's building orgasm by kissing her inner thighs and licking her navel.

"Come ride Daddy's dick."

Candice straddled him, and her lips were drawn to his like a magnet. He spread her ass cheeks to dig deeper inside her.

"How deep do you want me to go, Candice?"

"Deep, Daddy! Go deep!"

"I'll go as deep as you fuckin' want me to go." He groaned against her neck.

Candice rubbed her breasts as she stared down at him. Jasmine sauntered over and curled her tongue to flick her right nipple. Candice palmed the back of Jasmine's head to keep them both doing what they were doing. One fucking her, the other sucking her.

"Yes! Shit! Ooooh shit!" she moaned.

Jasmine palmed her ass and then smacked it, encouraging her to fuck Julian faster. Enjoying the sight before her eyes, Jasmine rubbed her sensitive areas. She placed one finger inside her pussy and slid another down the crack of Candice's ass. She looked into Julian's eyes and saw he couldn't hold out much longer.

"I wanna suck Daddy's dick," she purred.

Candice looked back at her and smiled. She lifted herself off Julian while Jasmine came face to face with his dick. Candice put his hard dick inside Jasmine's mouth and watched her suck on it like her favorite lollipop. Jasmine rubbed up his thigh as she sucked on his dick, forcing more into her mouth than she knew she could take.

"Mmm, yeah, suck it just like that," Candice coached.

She admired the way Jasmine's mouth worked. She had a serious gift. Jasmine flashed her eyes up at Julian with spit hanging from her lips.

"I can taste her pussy on your dick."

"Good," he groaned.

Candice sat back and played with her pussy, watching them enjoy each other. As soon as Julian penetrated her roomie, she felt her clit throb. Jasmine's moans rang through her ears, only getting her pussy wetter.

"I wanna feel all of you inside me!"

"You want Daddy to dig that pussy out?" he asked, pumping inside her.

"Go deep, Daddy! Yes! Oh my God, I feel it in my fuckin' stomach! Don't stop!" she begged.

Feeling his weight on top of her as he plowed into her turned Jasmine on more and more. She arched her back and panted until her mouth went dry while her body jerked. Seconds later, Candice came, and Julian followed suit.

"Mmm, fuck!" he groaned, releasing his seed into Jasmine.

The three collapsed on the plush bed, intertwining themselves in the silk sheets. Julian lay in the middle while Candice and Jasmine populated opposite sides of him. Candice could still feel her body quaking from the aftershocks of her multiple orgasms. She couldn't think of a time when she felt refreshed and relaxed. Although her body was tired, she thought she could take on the world. As soon as she got comfortable, she closed her eyes and drifted off to sleep when a male voice called her name.

"Candice?"

She blinked her eyes a few times, trying to escape the haze she'd been in. "D—Dimitri?"

He eyed her naked body up and down, and she could've fallen through the floorboards. "Funny seeing you here."

Chapter Fifteen

Candice's forehead creased, and her armpits started to moisten. She didn't know if it was embarrassment or nervousness in his presence.

"I could say the same to you," she muttered.

"Who's your friend, Candy?" Jasmine asked, stroking her arm with the back of her finger.

"Um—"

"Dimitri," he answered, cutting her off. "We go to school together."

"Oh really? I'm Jasmine, her... roommate. Nice to meet you," she replied, extending her hand.

He tipped his chin. "The pleasure is all mine."

"So, what are the three of you getting into for the rest of the night?"

Julian stepped up. "This is an invitation-only type of thing. You understand, don't you?"

Dimitri nodded and flashed a quick smile before turning his attention back to Candice.

"Yeah, I do. Maybe I'll just see you around. You still have my number, right?"

"Yeah, I do."

Candice watched him walk away, then turned back to Julian. "Why'd you do that?"

"Do what?"

"You know what. That was rude."

"Was it?" he asked calmly.

She sucked her teeth while bobbing her head. Feeling the tension brewing between the three of them, Jasmine interjected. "It was kind of rude, baby. But listen, Candy, I think Julian was trying to say that what we have here is golden. We don't know him, that's all."

"You didn't know me either at first, and now look at us," she pressed back.

"I won't speak for Julian, but as much as I want you to just be with us, I'm not going to get mad if you wanna go out there and do your own thing. Exploration can be fun."

"Jasmine is right. You have every right to explore, but it doesn't mean either of us has to be happy about it," Julian added.

Candice eyed the two of them, not for the words coming out of their mouths, but for their body language. She could tell neither wanted to let her go, but they had no control over what she did or who she did it with. All they could do was respect it.

"I'll be back."

She wrapped herself in a silk black robe and then exited the room. Walking at least four feet ahead of her, she saw Dimitri.

"Dimitri, wait up." She waved.

He turned around and waited for her to catch up before speaking. "What's up?"

"I just wanted to apologize for what happened back there. That was rude."

"Nah, I didn't take it like that, but thank you."

"Yeah, no problem."

The two of them stood in the middle of the floor and let the sounds of moans, rattling chains, and whipping fill the space between them.

"I still can't believe I saw you here, of all places. This is way different from running into you at the grocery store or somewhere other than a place like this," she admitted.

"Yeah, you're right. But what exactly do you see this '*place*' as?" he asked, making air quotes with his fingers.

"Uh, I don't know. I mean, it's my first time coming. But just from looking around, I guess it's a place where people can live out their fantasies and relish in their fetishes, right?"

"Yeah, but it's a little more than that to me."

"What do you mean?"

"I'm not only a member. I'm an investor."

"As in?"

"As in, I'm one-fourth of the owners of this place," he told her.

"I'm sorry, what? And how old are you again?"

"I'm twenty-five, and before you ask, I'm a grad student. I don't think I told you that before."

"And you just randomly decided to invest money into... this?" she asked, looking around.

"While most people I went to undergrad with chose to blow their refund checks on big screen TVs and lavish spring break vacations, I saved them up and decided to invest when the opportunity came my way. It's been such a hit that not only have I paid off all my student loan debt, but I've made a significant ROI."

"ROI?" she asked, scrunching her forehead.

"Return on investment." He chuckled.

"I'm sorry, I'm a business major."

"Wow... I'm shocked but impressed."

"Not as shocked as I was to see you here. Don't take this the wrong way, but I didn't peg you for the type of girl who would be caught dead here."

Candice folded her arms across her chest and tilted her head. "And just exactly what type of girl did you peg me for? A *goodie two shoes*?" she asked, returning the air quotes.

"Exactly."

She shrugged. "Well, I'm sorry to have disappointed you."

"Oh, trust me. There's no disappointment at all. If anything, I like you more now than I did when we first met."

Candice's eyes flashed up to meet his. He had a pair of dark brown eyes that had the power to make any girl get lost in them. She didn't figure she was any different. Before she could speak up, he leaned into her cheek and whispered, "You smell amazing, by the way."

She blushed and took a step back. "Thank you... you smell good, too."

"Do you need to get back to your... friends, or will you allow me to steal more of your time?"

Candice looked back at the room where Jasmine and Julian were both sitting on the bed, staring a hole into her back. She quickly turned around and shook her head. "No, everything is fine. Steal away."

"Cool. You mind if I show you around?"

"Sure."

Chapter Sixteen

The two of them made their way down the dimly lit hallway passing by rooms with only sheer curtains separating the people in the midst of acting out their fantasies and the onlookers outside. She wasn't accustomed to people openly putting their sexual acts on display for the world to see. It was like being in a real-life porn flick.

There was a woman with her knees embedded into the satin sheets underneath her with a gag in her mouth. Candice could see the drool pooling at the corners. A man was in front of her, making her crawl forward to him as he walked backward with a whip in his hand.

"So, anyone can just walk up and watch?" Candice whispered to Dimitri while stopping in her tracks.

"Pretty much. We have sort of an open-door policy here," he told her as he ran the back of his finger down her arm.

Without responding, she simply nodded, and the two of them continued down the hallway. Every few seconds, her eyes would take in something she'd never seen. Three rooms down, there was a woman with colorful, blinking Christmas lights tied around her ankles and wrists. The man in the room wore a mask and attempted to insert a butt plug inside her while getting his dick sucked.

"Wow," she muttered, stopping yet again.

She felt terrible for awkwardly gawking at the sight in front of her, but she couldn't help herself.

"Is that something you'd like to try?"

"Me? No way. I've barely just gotten comfortable doing the things I'm doing now."

"And exactly what are you doing, Candice?"

"I'm almost one hundred percent sure you saw me. You're a smart man. Put two and two together."

"So, you enjoy being with women and men?"

"I enjoy being with her and him. That's it."

"That's it as in you've found your comfort zone, or that's it as in they are the only two you've been with?"

"Both. This may be hard to believe, but I was a virgin when I met them."

Dimitri tipped his head. "I see, and no, that's not hard to believe. Does that mean you'd never consider being with anyone else? Male or female?"

She looked up at him again, seeing the passion sizzling in his eyes for her. She blushed and looked down at her feet. "I don't know...no one else has presented themselves to me in that way before, male or female."

"And what if I did? Would you turn me down?"

Heat flushed over her entire body. She could feel the lust burning inside her as her curiosity heightened. She'd never wondered what being with someone other than Julian would be like. Now knowing the ins and outs of his and Jasmine's relationship, Candice wondered just how long the threesome would remain three before other people were folded into the mix.

"I-I—"

"Shh," he hissed, placing his fingertip against his full lips. He gently pushed Candice against the wall and pressed his body against hers. "You don't have to give me an answer right now...no pressure. Just know I want you, and I'm down to do whatever you want me to do to your body. Wherever, whenever."

She had never thought about being with another man before. She was nervous, but the jolts surging through her pussy were more than enough to put those fears aside.

"Kiss me," she begged, unable to hide the heat between her thighs for him.

Hovering over her, Dimitri leaned down and pressed his lips against hers. As soon as the kiss ended, Candice couldn't stop blushing and smiling like a teenager who'd just had her first kiss.

"Can I ask you something?" she asked, slowly pulling away.

He shot her a quick nod. "Anything."

"What made you want to invest in this?"

"I love sex. I've always loved sex. I think it's the most freeing yet intimate thing shared between people. There are hundreds of thousands of kinks in the world and fantasies that people just want to check off their bucket lists. Why not capitalize on that while ensuring everyone has a safe and fun time?"

Candice nodded. "Smart... I see why you're a business major now."

"I know you said it was your first time here, but do you see yourself returning?"

"Yeah, I mean, don't get me wrong, I was overwhelmed at first, but I've had a good first experience here."

"Would you like to have an even better time?" he asked, slightly cocking his head to the side.

"Are you asking me to sleep with you tonight, Dimitri?"

"I would love the opportunity to show you things you've never experienced, but only if you're comfortable. Everything we do here is one hundred percent consensual."

Dimitri eyed Candice's body language closely. Although she hadn't directly given him a yes or a no, he knew she wanted him. He also knew she was afraid. Her inhibitions were holding her back from what he knew would be one of the most mind-blowing experiences of her young adult life.

"Do me a favor," he said while resting his hands on the peak of her shoulders.

"What?"

"Close your eyes."

Candice's eyes fell shut. "Okay, now what?"

"I want you to think about something you probably would never see yourself doing in your waking life, but you've thought about it... fantasized about it... even touched yourself about it."

With her eyes slammed shut, Candice began to think. She'd never thought about being with a woman, *check*. She'd also never thought about being with a man and a woman simultaneously, *check*.

"Hmm...I—I don't know," she mumbled.

"Think a little harder. I'm sure there's something. It's okay to be selfish, Candice. You can have anything you want here."

"Anything?" she asked as her eyebrow perked up.

"Yes, anything," he assured her.

"What if I told you I wanted to be with you and them too?"

"Like a foursome?"

She nodded slowly. "Yeah, I guess so."

"Is this what you want?" he asked.

"Yes... if I can have it all here, then I want it all."

Chapter Seventeen

Dimitri stepped forward and placed both hands on her face to pull her lips onto his. It only took seconds before Candice felt his tongue slip between her lips. Things would be perfect if only his tongue were between her other set. Dimitri slowly ran his hands down her petite frame. She parted them with ease as soon as he got to her thighs, and he slipped a finger between her warmth.

"Did you know the clitoris has over eight thousand nerve endings? That's why it's so simple to make you tremble when I touch it," he whispered as he massaged her button.

A low whimper slipped past Candice's lips. She could feel her pussy getting wetter and wetter for him with just the stroke of his finger. If he drove her that crazy with his hand, she didn't know if she would be able to handle the real thing.

"Let's go," she told him.

The two walked back to the room where Jasmine and Julian were. As soon as Candice appeared, Jasmine sat up and smiled.

"Hey," she said.

"Hey." Candice breathed while walking over to her.

She quickly placed her lips onto Jasmine's and intertwined her tongue with hers. As surprised as Jasmine was, there was no way she could resist Candice's touch. The two continued to kiss slowly as

Jasmine gently glided her hand over Candice's exposed thigh. Knowing exactly what time it was, she quickly slid her hand in between her legs and felt her warmth as she pushed the tips of two of her fingers inside her.

Candice eagerly slid the robe off her body, exposing her breasts to everyone in the room, but only locking eyes with Jasmine. Jasmine licked her lips and ran her fingertips over her roommate's hard nipples, then hungrily sucked on each of them. Without delay, Candice crawled on the bed and spread her legs from east to west. Jasmine began licking the soft folds of her pussy gently as she flattened her tongue across Candice's clit. Candice tossed her head back and began to run her fingers wildly through her hair.

"Ooh, shit," she moaned as her eyes glanced at Dimitri. His dick stood at attention as he silently watched her.

She looked down and watched Jasmine lap her pussy. As good as it felt, she was ready to take Dimitri for a test drive.

"Wanna join?" Candice purred.

Dimitri and Julian both made their way over to the girls. Julian propped Jasmine's ass up and started eating her pussy from behind. Dimitri lowered himself beside Jasmine, and the two took turns lapping Candice's sweet spot, which almost drove her crazy.

"Shiiiiiiiittttttt! That's it right there! Don't stop!" Candice squealed.

Soon, both Dimitri and Jasmine had a sheen of Candice's sweet excretions on their lips.

Wanting more, Dimitri greedily licked his lips and then stood to his feet to hover over Candice. As soon as he exposed himself to her, she reached out and started jacking off his long, hard dick, then took the tip into her warm mouth.

Jasmine began sucking Julian's dick while Candice lapped at her pussy from behind. With Candice's ripe pussy right before him, Dimitri spat on the tip of his dick and slowly entered Candice's pussy from the back.

"Ooooh shit," Candice squealed, gasping for air, then looked back at Dimitri.

He bit his lip as he took long, slow strokes inside her. She'd secretly been anticipating the pain of being penetrated again, but was pleasantly surprised that she felt nothing but pleasure with Dimitri inside her. She could feel his dick swelling with every slow stroke, filling her right up. Candice flashed her eyes up at Julian, who couldn't take his eyes off her. He enjoyed watching her get fucked while eating Jasmine's pussy at the same time.

Julian would be the first to admit his reservations about bringing another man into the bedroom. The three of them worked like a well-oiled machine, but having Dimitri there only brought out more of the freak in Candice he knew she'd been hiding all along.

"Mmm, does it feel good, baby?" Jasmine asked as she ran her tongue up and down his shaft and flicked the head of his dick with her tongue.

Julian tightly gripped a handful of her hair and forced his dick deeper down her throat. He locked his eyes on Candice as she sucked on Jasmine's enlarged clit. She more Candice licked, the more of his dick he forced down Jasmine's throat. Not wanting to cum, he broke his trance and slid his dick between Jasmine's jaws.

Lying side by side, Candice and Jasmine were both being fucked. Candice was in the missionary position, while Jasmine was fucked doggy style.

"Ooh, fuck! Right there, Daddy!" Jasmine moaned as she reached over and took one of Candice's bouncing breasts into her mouth and sucked on it. She stared into her eyes as she sucked on her hard mounds. Wanting to feel every bit of pleasure, Candice pulled Jasmine's lips onto hers, and the two began moaning in each other's mouths.

"Does it feel good, Candy? Is he fucking you good?" Jasmine asked.

"Mmhm. It feels soooo good!" she screamed, her head tossed back in ecstasy. She could feel Dimitri fucking her into a sexual coma.

Jasmine ran her hand down the outline of Candice's smooth thigh and looked up at Dimitri. "My turn."

Dimitri slowly slid his dick out of Candice and turned to Jasmine. She quickly pulled his long piece into her mouth and started sucking on it.

"Mmm, shit. It tastes so sweet," Jasmine purred.

Julian grabbed Candice by the hand and helped her off the bed. She dropped to her knees as he stood over her and began sucking his dick. Julian let his head fall back, and his eyes close for the first time all night. He felt Candice's hands roam over his hard chest and muscles as her wet lips sucked him.

"Mmm, fuck," he growled while latching his hand around the back of her neck.

He cracked open his eyes to see Jasmine riding Dimitri's dick and quickly pulled Candice back to her feet. He'd been waiting for what seemed like a lifetime to be inside her again. With her body suspended in the air, Julian lowered her petite body down on his dick and slowly slid his length in and out of her.

"Mmmm." She trembled.

"Can you handle it?" he whispered in her ear.

"Y—yes." She shook.

"Tell Daddy how good it feels, Candy."

"It feels soooo fuck—fuckin' good."

Julian began picking up the pace. He wanted to pound her pussy until it was so sore she could barely walk.

"Fuckkkkkkkk! I'm about t-to—I'm cumming!" Candice yelled out.

Julian gently laid her down on the bed and started eating her pussy. Dimitri followed suit and flipped Jasmine onto her back, burying his head between her thighs. She quickly palmed the back of his head, enjoying the feeling.

"Don't stop! Don't stop! I'm gonna cum!" Jasmine demanded.

Candice looked over at Jasmine. She loved watching her cum. Her hands extended and roamed all over her roomie's full breasts. They looked so suckable that her mouth watered, just staring at them.

"Come sit on my face, Jas," Candice demanded.

Jasmine threw her leg over and climbed onto Candice's face, hovering her pussy over her lips. Candice licked her lips and gripped Jasmine's ass, pulling her pussy lips down on her tongue. Without hesitation, Jasmine began rolling her hips against Candice's firm tongue, ready to bust again.

"Grab my ass while you eat my pussy! Mmm, yes! Fuck! Yes, you want my cum all over your pretty little face? Is that what you want?" Jasmine said through gritted teeth.

Candice moaned as she continued tongue fucking her roommate's pussy and massaging her soft ass. Jasmine reached back to play with Candice's pussy as Dimitri and Julian sucked her nipples simultaneously.

Unable to hold her climax back, she came the hardest she'd ever cum in her life. "Mmm, fuck!!!!"

Jasmine's pussy throbbed as she slowly climbed off Candice's face. Dimitri reached out and slowly started caressing her pussy with one hand while stroking his dick with the other. As physically spent as her body was, Jasmine still had some juice left in her, and she was determined to give the night her all. She started sucking his dick while jacking off Julian simultaneously.

Candice crawled behind her and began kissing her neck lightly. She ran her fingertips from Jasmine's neck, over the cliff of her shoulders and over her hard nipples. An electric jolt surged through her body as Candice's soft fingertips kneaded her nipples.

"See how much trouble you're getting me into?" Candice whispered in her ear, then sucked on the lobe.

Jasmine quickly turned to her and grabbed the back of her head while shoving her tongue deep inside her mouth. Everything about Candice turned her on to the max. She pushed Candice back against the bed, lifted her legs in the air, and spread her juicy pussy lips open to slide her tongue over her throbbing clit.

Candice's hands clenched the bedsheets as her body jerked forward. "Ooooh shit, Jas!"

Jasmine's tongue shifted around inside Candice's pussy while she tugged on her nipples. Julian slid his dick back inside Jasmine while Dimitri began sucking on Candice's firm nipples. She quickly palmed the back of Jasmine and Dimitri's heads to keep them right where they were at. She was about to have the climax of a lifetime.

"Ooooh my fuck—fucking God!" Her body shook.

Dimitri climbed off the bed and swung Candice's lifeless legs over to the edge of the bed. He eyed Jasmine, who made her way over to him and sat on her knees. He slid his dick inside Candice, fucking her pussy with no mercy. After a few strokes, Jasmine slid his dick out of Candice, sucked on it, and then slid it back inside.

"Mmm, fuck," Dimitri groaned.

He'd had his share of foursomes in the past, but nothing compared to his experience with Candice, Julian, and Jasmine. The four of them were forces to be reckoned with in the bedroom. Jasmine crawled over to Julian. He was getting his dick sucked by Candice when she started licking his balls.

Dimitri flipped Candice over onto her stomach and smacked her ass so hard that he left a red mark in the form of a handprint. Candice looked back at him and bit her bottom lip seductively. "Again!" she demanded.

Dimitri began pounding into her pussy and smacking her ass like there was no tomorrow.

"Mmm, fuck! Yes! Yessss!" Candice moaned.

He continued fucking her from the back while she and Jasmine sucked Julian's dick. He watched them take turns sucking the head, licking up the shaft, and sucking on his ball sack. Julian had the palms of his hands planted on the back of both of their heads. Dimitri tossed his head back, feeling his climax surging through the soles of his feet.

He quickly slid out of Candice and spun her body around to face him. Candice and Jasmine fell to their knees in front of Julian and Dimitri as they jacked off until they came, sprinkling their cum all over their protruding tongues.

Jasmine leaned over and kissed Candice, swirling her tongue inside her mouth.

Candice couldn't help but smile as the events of the night danced through her head. She'd gone from being a shy virgin to a bonafide freak in the blink of an eye. *This is something I could get used to,* she thought.

THE END

Afterword

Reader,

Thank you for reading *Bi-Curious.* If you've made it this far, I hope you'll consider taking a minute to tell me what you thought about the book in the form of a **book review and/or rating**. Don't hesitate to let me know what you'd like to see from me next! I thoroughly enjoy reading your thoughts and hearing from you as well! I'm always striving to attract new readers and retain current ones, and reviews are one of the easiest ways to attract readers. If you loved the book, tell a friend, and most importantly, let me know!

All my love,
K.L. Hall

About the Author

K.L. Hall is a national bestselling and award-winning author. As a serial storyteller, Hall has penned over three dozen titles in various genres—including African American urban fiction and romance, paranormal, children's books (as Kimberley M.), and non-fiction. Her fictional stories straddle the intersection of classic Urban and spell-binding Romance.

Highly Acclaimed Titles:

In the Arms of a Savage: (Peaked at #1 in Women's Fiction)

The Potomac Falls Series (Peaked at #1 and #2 in African American Erotica)

Sign up for my mailing list to stay updated with new releases, giveaways, sneak peeks, and more! Click this link: https://bit.ly/38RMpV5

Connect with me on social media:

Facebook: https://www.facebook.com/authorklhall

Twitter: https://twitter.com/authorklhall

Instagram: https://www.instagram.com/officialklhall/

Website: https://www.authorklhall.com

Also by K.L. Hall

Novels:

Diary of a Hood Princess 1-3

Rise of a Street King: The Justice Silva Story *(Spin-Off to the Diary of a Hood Princess series)*

Broken Condoms and Promises 1-3

In the Arms of a Savage 1-3

Built for a Savage: Blaze and Camille's Love Story *(Spin-Off to the In the Arms of a Savage Series)*

A Ruthle$$ Love Story 1-3

Fallin' for the Alpha of the Streets 1-2

The Most Savage of Them All: The Wolfe Calloway Story *(Prequel to the In the Arms of a Savage Series)*

When a Gangsta Loves a Good Girl

Caught Between my Husband and a Hustler

The Illest Taboo 1-2

To the Only Thug I'll Ever Love

A Lover's Heist: Chief and Gianna's Love Story

A Lover's Heist II: Rome and Lira's Love Story

A Lover's Heist III: Baby and Skai's Love Story

Crushed Velvet & Cashmere

Crushed Velvet & Cashmere 2

Entanglements

Short Reads + Novellas:

Bi-Curious: An Erotic Tale

Bi-Curious 2: Tastes Like Candy

House of Cards 1-2

A Savage Calloway Christmas *(Christmas novella to the In the Arms of a Savage Series)*

Lovin' the Alpha of the Streets: A Valentine's Day Novella *(Valentine's Day novella to the Fallin' for the Alpha of the Streets Series)*

Awakened: A Paranormal Romance

As Long as You Stay Down

Solace in Seven

Solace II: The Final Cut

Something Bleu

Something Borrowed

Something New

The Knight Before Christmas: A Potomac Falls Short

I'll Be Home for Christmas: A Potomac Falls Short Book II

Triggered: A Potomac Falls Novella

Children's Books:

Princess for Hire

Princess Twinkle Toes & the Missing Magic Sneakers

Little One, Change the World

Adjust Your Crown: A Self-Love Coloring Book for Children of Color

Non-Fiction:

Authors are a Business: The Booked & Busy Course Mini Book

www.ingramcontent.com/pod-product-compliance
Ingram Content Group UK Ltd.
Pitfield, Milton Keynes, MK11 3LW, UK
UKHW022012190726
13853UKWH00004B/1894

9 798986 376189